Legacy

A phone call from a desperate young woman to John Leith, an Edinburgh accountant, is both intriguing and worrying, and when she disappears he is concerned for her safety. While trying to trace her he is threatened by a man who owns a Harley Davidson motorbike. Is he the girl's boyfriend or simply the reason why she is so frightened? John, using the resources of the Sentinel Agency in an attempt to solve the mystery, is soon involved in an incident where another young girl is injured by a speeding car; but was it an accident?

The biker, who always hides his features behind the visor of his helmet, has a partner and the two become aggressive instead of just using threats. John's car is tampered with, nearly causing a fatal crash, and after other such attempts on his life, he begins to piece together the clues that point in only one direction, to the identity of the criminals and the reason for their desperate attempts to make him stop the investigation. John Leith refuses to be put off by their tactics and the tale builds up to a violent confrontation, and a surprising revelation.

by the same author

DOUBLE ENTRY

MARGARET McKINLAY

Legacy

THE CRIME CLUB
An Imprint of HarperCollins *Publishers*

First published in Great Britain in 1993
by The Crime Club, an imprint of
HarperCollins Publishers, 77–85 Fulham Palace Road,
Hammersmith, London W6 8JB

9 8 7 6 5 4 3 2 1

Margaret McKinlay asserts the moral right to be identified
as the author of this work.

A catalogue record for this book is
available from the British Library

ISBN 0 00 232426 1

Photoset in Linotron Baskerville by
Rowland Phototypesetting Ltd
Bury St Edmunds, Suffolk
Printed and bound in Great Britain by
HarperCollins Book Manufacturing, Glasgow

To my husband Patrick, my children Frances, Patricia and John, and for James

And with thanks to Harry, Peter, Alan, John and Alvin's, the experts

CHAPTER 1

The phone call couldn't have come at a worse time and John only answered it because the efficient Val was out for her lunch. The voice in his ear sounded muffled and it took a few seconds for him to realize that the female caller was crying.

He took a deep breath. 'Look, I can't hear what you're saying. Let's start again.' He didn't mean to sound abrupt but in a way it seemed to steady the girl and the next time she spoke he could make out what she was saying, although her voice still wobbled.

'Can I see you? I must speak to you,' she pleaded.

It made no sense. 'Are you sure you've got the right number—this is John Leith, Kramer Property.' Had the switchboard put through a call that was meant for the Sentinel Security agency on the floor below?

'I know.' It was a hurried cry of desperation. 'I heard about Mr Kramer dying—I would have spoken to him— now I don't know what to do.'

'Just tell me who you are and how my uncle could have helped you,' John said, but then he was aware of another voice in the background, a man's voice and it sounded angry. The girl had put her hand over the receiver and the conversation became distant, a blurred murmur.

'Hello?' John waited but then he heard what sounded like a sharp cry of pain and the other end of the phone clattered down. He put his own phone down slowly, wondering who the girl had been and if she would call back. The memory of her desperation troubled him on and off all afternoon, but the more dominant thoughts were of the funeral service he had to attend the next day and the effect his uncle's death would have on his own future.

*

Rees Kramer's funeral was as private as the man himself had been in life. Only four mourners heard the graveside prayers uttered by the Presbyterian minister who had never met the dead man. And John found the impersonal words more chilling than the bloom of damp that had formed on his uncle's coffin in the freezing March mist.

The two women were dry-eyed. His sister Gwen had her arm around Janet, his uncle's middle-aged housekeeper. Tollis, business partner and friend of Rees for many years, stood stony-faced. Then it was all over with almost indecent haste, as if the reverend gentleman was as anxious as the rest of them to reach the warmth of the waiting cars.

Their feet crunched on the gravel path where weeds and long grass had blurred its margins. Each blade of grass was heavy with moisture and the cypress trees, which seemed a feature of cemeteries, dripped.

John shivered. 'We're all coming back to Elmwood with you,' he told Janet. She was wearing a grey tweed coat that he'd seen many times before and a matching fluffy woollen beret. She had scorned the wearing of black because she was certain that Rees wouldn't expect it.

'There's no need,' she said with calmness. 'I don't mind going back to an empty house. Rees spent so many nights at the Edinburgh flat that I got used to my own company.'

'We're coming anyway,' John said, letting the two women walk ahead while he fell into step with Tollis.

'I thought Rees would have preferred cremation,' Tollis growled. He had his hands deep in the pockets of a dark overcoat, his broad shoulders hunched up around his neck. 'It doesn't fit somehow—Rees mouldering under wet clay.'

John knew exactly what he meant. Rees had liked clear-cut decisions and cremation would have been a neater ending, but his uncle had left instructions which included 'no flowers'. They'd all bought wreaths anyway and there had been an elaborate one in the shape of a cross 'from the staff of Kramers'. He glanced back and saw that the grave-diggers were already filling in the hole and beyond them he saw another figure, a woman in a duffle coat.

'Wonder who that is?' he said. She had stepped forward to pause beside the grave and now she was looking towards them, as if she wanted to join them on the path. Tollis screwed up his eyes, then shook his head.

'Can't see her clearly with that hood up. Someone wanting to pay her last respects without intruding, I suppose.'

The minister had driven off by the time they reached Tollis's car, which was parked just inside the gates. The two men stood aside to let the women get into the back and as John was about to slide into the passenger seat, he saw the uninvited guest walking down the path towards them out of the low-lying mist. He could see her more clearly now. She was quite young, dumpy, with two long strands of dark hair straggling out of the hood to lie on the front of the duffle coat. She walked heavily in flat-soled boots, her breath streaming out to mix with the dampness that was rolling across the cemetery. Was she someone who knew Rees and had read the notice of the funeral in the paper? If so, she knew that it was to be a private affair and that would account for her standing well back. And somehow it gave the bleak day a softer touch, to know that someone liked Rees enough to attend unobtrusively and pay her last respects. He saw Tollis glance in her direction too before he drove off.

It was with mixed feelings that he got out of the car at Elmwood, the house that he'd lived in from the age of ten when his uncle had taken on the role of parent to Gwen and him. Always, Elmwood had been warm and welcoming although it was quite a large old place. It had the air of being cared for and therefore seemed to pass that caring on to whoever visited it. None of that was due to Rees Kramer particularly, because he disliked visitors invading his privacy, but the house itself seemed to have a solid reliability in its mellow cream stone. Now the house belonged to John and so did the Kramer business. The will had not yet been read but he knew that Gwen was to receive a settlement while he was expected to take over running the company.

'It's not what you'd planned, is it?' Tollis commented

drily as they stood in what had been Rees's study, each holding a good measure of Scotch.

It wasn't how he'd seen his future. Rees had seemed to be on the mend after a heart attack, but then another massive coronary had struck him down and it had ended his life in seconds.

'What are you going to do?' Tollis went on, blunt as usual.

John shook his head. 'I've had a taste of running the business in these last few months but it's been going on its own momentum. The heads of departments know more about the business than I do and there is so much I have to learn. Being an accountant is a help, but I should be a chartered surveyor at least. I suppose the first step will be to get the managers together for a discussion and see how they see things going in the future. Kramer Property is in for a quiet period at the very least until things settle down.'

His words sounded sensible but they gave no hint of the sheer panic he was feeling. So many jobs depended on what he did next and the initial impulse to sell off the lot was not the answer.

Tollis had tossed his overcoat across a leather chair and now he sank deep in its twin. He regarded John thoughtfully but with a tinge of sympathy as well, as if he knew what he had been thinking. 'At least my side of the business is separate. Rees signed over Sentinel Security to me some years ago, as you know, but any decisions you make could still affect me since we share the same building. Sentinel has always been associated with Kramer's and in most people's minds Rees was still in charge of the lot. It made life difficult at times.' He looked at John through narrowed eyes. 'I had hopes that you would join my side of the firm but I suppose that's impossible now.'

He sounded regretful and John wanted to ask him not to dismiss the idea because it was what he'd been considering himself. It was on the tip of his tongue to tell Tollis to suspend any decision about the future but he said nothing. The responsibility that had landed in his lap because of his uncle's death couldn't be dumped on someone else. There was no one else. He changed the subject.

'I had a strange phone call yesterday from a woman who seemed to be in trouble—she was under the impression that Rees could have helped her but I didn't get the whole story.'

Tollis was reaching for his coat. 'If it was important she'll phone again,' he said.

'Aren't you staying for lunch?' John asked, but Tollis shook his head. 'I've got appointments for this afternoon. Business is a bit slack and pretty boring—just routine stuff coming in from solicitors looking for witnesses and the like. It's usual for the time of year.' He drained the last of the whisky before going on. 'Security is not on people's minds at the end of winter for some reason. Pop in if you feel the need for light relief.'

'Or to escape,' John said with feeling, and Tollis grunted something close to a chuckle before leaving.

There was a feeling of anti-climax in the house. The funeral had been hanging over them for days and now that it was over none of them knew what to do with themselves. In the end it was Janet who spoke positively.

'I'll stay on for a while. I'm going to live with my sister in Inverness eventually, but not just yet,' she said as they drank coffee after lunch. 'Will you live here?' she went on and it got right down to the nitty-gritty of his future which had been unsettled for months anyway.

'I expect I will,' he said, because selling Elmwood was not something to think about yet and before Rees's death he was already in the process of selling his flat so that he could buy a house.

'I need more space for David when he comes home from school at weekends or the holidays. I'm glad you'll still be here.'

'Och, David will be eight this year and he'll bring friends home—it won't matter who feeds him or does the house-work. Of course, if you had a wife there would be no prob-lem at all,' she said drily as she got up and began to clear the table. 'My sister has a little shop and I might go and help her with it, but I'm in no hurry. Rees set up a nice pension for me and I'll be very comfortable.'

'What about you, Gwen?' John asked his sister.

'Well, the boys are coming home to Aberdeen for Easter next week. I'll stay for a few more days though, and give Janet a hand.'

'And you should have gone back to town with Tollis,' Janet told him quietly as she stacked plates. 'Gwen and I have a lot of clearing out to do, Rees's clothes and things, and we can get all that done before you need to move in here. Stay at the flat in town and sort yourself out with the business.'

Both women looked at him expectantly and he didn't need much persuasion.

'OK. You win, I'll drive into town.'

It was a relief to have something to do and he didn't want to be around when Gwen and Janet were turning out Rees's belongings. Not that his uncle was the sort of man who kept souvenirs or photograph albums; Rees had lived a tidy life and that included keeping his emotions in sealed compartments. No, there would be no treasured souvenirs, nothing to tug at the heartstrings, just essential papers, deeds to property, insurance policies and the last will and testament. All sorted out long ago to save anyone else the trouble. It would make a suitable epitaph, he thought, as he drove along the coast road to the city. Rees Kramer, a tidy man who gave no love and expected none; a man who burdened no one with his personal affairs. Tollis, who knew him better than anyone wouldn't argue with that.

He felt the difference the minute he set foot in the Kramer office block. The girls at the reception desks smiled in quite a different way, sympathetic but respectful at the same time, but that might have been because he was still dressed in his sober funeral suit instead of his usual casual clothes.

Or perhaps it was because up to now he had been seen as a stand-in, the temporary boss, who would be gone once

Rees took over the reins again. Only Rees was not coming back and now the inexperienced nephew who was only thirty-two was in control and their jobs were at risk. Was that what they would all be thinking?

'We didn't expect you today,' said Val, Rees's assistant, and even she was more formal. They'd got to know each other during the infrequent days he'd felt obliged to visit the office while Rees was ill, but now the scenario had changed and like everyone else in the building she was wondering how the change would affect her.

She was a calm woman in her mid-thirties who knew exactly how Rees ran the business, so she'd coordinated things efficiently in the emergency. However, there would come a time when management decisions had to be made and Val couldn't do that for him.

'I wish we'd known you were coming in because there was a young woman asking for you and reception said she refused to leave her name. She said she was at the funeral this morning . . .' Val's eyebrows were raised.

'Yes, there was someone there but . . . Did she say what she wanted?'

Val shook her head. 'She was very upset about something, but she wouldn't give any details.' She paused as if she was going to elaborate and then thought better of it. 'The girls told her to try phoning for an appointment— they weren't sure of your plans,' she explained.

First the girl had phoned the office after learning that Rees was dead, and she'd sounded very scared. Then she'd attended his funeral, now this . . . He had a feeling that she wouldn't give up. 'Tell the exchange that I want to speak to her if she does call, and if I'm not here to be sure to make an appointment.' There was nothing else he could do until he knew what she wanted.

The novelty of sitting at Rees's desk had worn off in the last months, but today it felt strange all over again, probably because of the funeral. He took a deep breath and tried to resign himself to a whole new lifestyle. Val waited, but if she knew what he was thinking, her expression didn't reveal it.

'Right. I need some advice and it's time for honesty,' he told her bluntly. 'What is the general feeling about me taking over the business? You must get feedback from some of the departments. I need to know what morale is like—and sit down for goodness' sake and forget for a moment that we're in the office.'

'Uncertainty, I suppose.' She ignored the chairs around a low coffee table and pulled an upright one forward. She crossed her legs and adjusted her skirt, hesitating about giving an opinion, he assumed, but she wouldn't have lasted long with Rees if she hadn't been able to analyse a situation, so he waited.

'I think most people are waiting for you to consult. A few have been looking at the vacancies in the paper—' and here she smiled—'but not seriously—yet—mainly because they're prepared to wait and see what happens next.'

Her eyes were twinkling behind her sensible spectacles but what she said made sense. 'Surely there's no rush? Why not go on as we have been doing? We won't slide into ruin yet a while.'

John leaned back in his uncle's swivel chair and felt the soft leather give under him. The seat moulded itself to his body as if it was designed for him, but it would take more than good design before he could fill his uncle's shoes. 'Thank you. Now, is there anyone you would pick out as an overall manager?'

She blinked twice, as if the question came as a shock, and John guessed that for years she had acted as Rees's right hand but that he'd never given her the freedom to voice her own opinions.

'Manager?'

'It's only an option. You and I both know that I'm not ready for this and if the business isn't to go down the tubes, I'll need an expert to run things.'

'A manager,' she repeated, as if the thought of someone else taking over had not occurred to her.

'How long have you worked here, Val?' he asked quietly, studying her. She was not beautiful but she was attractive, with a quick intelligence in her grey eyes. She had neat fair hair, cut in a short style that was fashionable but he suspected it was chosen because it was easy to manage. She was slim, moved as discreetly as she dressed; exactly the sort of person who would have suited Rees's own personality.

He didn't know a thing about her life outside the office; not where she lived or even if she was married and suddenly he felt he should know these things.

'Since I left college,' she said simply. 'Sixteen years.'

'Then don't you think you're the best person to know who I can depend on? And would you put yourself forward as a candidate?'

She drew a deep breath. She was not the type to get wildly excited and if she did she would never show it, he thought.

'Yes. I know as much as Mr Kramer about the functions of each of the departments. I worked with Mr Kramer, who made the real decisions, and he wasn't a qualified surveyor.'

There was a hint of bitterness in her voice, and he wondered how long she had felt that she was being overlooked and even used by his uncle?

'But you didn't leave, you stuck it out when you could probably have got a managerial position somewhere else?'

'Maybe. But women don't walk into those jobs and here I was at least involved and paid an excellent salary.'

'Point taken.' There was silence while he digested what she'd said. She was right about knowing a great deal more than most about the running of the business, but Rees had not been an open sort of person. No matter how much Val had observed, she had not been privy to his uncle's thoughts, nor could there have been any discussion between them on how Rees saw the future of the business. So he couldn't automatically appoint her as overall manager, not immediately anyway. He would have to take his time to make that decision.

'I'll need your help for quite a bit, guidance about the other branches, etcetera, but I won't rush into changing anything. I'm glad you felt you could speak your mind.'

And already she had assumed her anonymous role of efficient assistant. She pulled it on like a mask but now he knew it was her safety-valve and that underneath it she was an executive trying to get out.

'And I've decided to keep a low profile for a bit, so for a start I'm going downstairs to Sentinel to see Tollis,' he said with a grin.

He used the back stairs, knowing it was a means of escaping—for a little while—to drop in on Tollis's untidy office, where files seemed to breed and multiply in corners.

'I wondered how long you'd last up there,' Tollis murmured. He'd already shed his suit jacket, his tie was pulled down and he had rolled up the sleeves of his white shirt. A cigarette burned away in a heaped ashtray as he offered strong coffee in a mug. 'As a matter of fact, I've got a new client coming in about ten minutes and you might like to sit in.'

And John felt himself relax in the sheer pleasurable anticipation of eavesdropping on Tollis's unpredictable business affairs. He moved papers from a worn leather chair and sat down with his long legs stretched out in front of him. 'You don't sound all that excited about it,' he said.

'It's only slightly more interesting than the other stuff that's been coming in but I'll let the young woman tell the whole story for herself. She's come over from Canada and I think she chose us after she stuck a pin in the list of private detectives in the yellow pages.'

John jerked upright. 'I wonder if it's the one who was at the cemetery this morning.'

'Hardly. What made you think that?'

'Because she came straight to Kramer's looking for me. The girls said she was very upset but they couldn't get anything out of her and I think she was the one on the phone yesterday.'

'Maybe she's a long-lost relation, come to contest the

will,' Tollis suggested dourly. 'If there are any around, this
is the time they'll appear—no doubt you'll find out soon
enough.'

'I hope so,' John said. Tollis had only had a glimpse of
her at the cemetery, he hadn't heard the sheer panic in the
girl's voice. 'I think she's in trouble.'

Tollis leaned his chin on the hand that held a cigarette
and looked with narrowed eyes at John through the tobacco
smoke. 'And you've got the smell of a mystery. You sure
can attract them,' he said as he heaved himself out of the
chair and shrugged on his jacket. He slipped his tie up to
his collar and ran his fingers through dark hair that was so
short it never needed to be combed. 'Right, let's see this
client in the interview room—I keep that tidy,' he said.

It was not the same girl. This one was tall, fair and
slender, possibly in her early twenties. She was also nervous. Tollis introduced himself and then John, and speaking softly, she told them her name was Maria Twarog.

'It's Polish,' she explained, 'but I was born in Canada.'
Her accent gave that away.

Tollis pulled out a chair for her. 'What can we do for
you, Maria?'

She sat on the edge of her seat, clutching a black leather
shoulder-bag, and at first didn't seem to know who to look
at, but in the end settled for John. Tollis drifted off to the
side of the room where he leaned against the wall with his
arms folded, leaving John to get on with it, but the girl was
still uneasy.

'Just take your time,' John said. She nodded and licked
her lips.

'My parents are dead but my great-aunt lived here, in
Edinburgh. She was related to my mother and her name
was Lucy Simpson—she was quite old. I met her only
twice, once when I came here on holiday with my mother
and once when she came to Canada. I knew that I would
inherit her property when she died, a house and some
money.' She paused, glanced over her shoulder at Tollis

and nervously moistened her lips. Tollis intervened at that point.

'I have something else to do so I'll leave Mr Leith to get the details. I'll send someone in with coffee,' and then he handed John a pad of scrap paper, raised his eyebrows in a gesture that said 'she doesn't want me around' and left the room. There was a pause as the door closed softly behind him.

'Maybe you don't deal with such small things,' she said, looking a lot more comfortable now. 'You see, my aunt promised me a painting and some other things and I'm not sure how to trace them.'

'The agency takes on all sorts of inquiries and recovering property is quite commonplace,' John assured her. 'Were these things in the will—have you spoken to her lawyer?'

'They were set aside when the house and the rest of her furniture were sold. The housekeeper was to look after them until I made arrangements to have them sent on, but she didn't answer my letters and I don't know her new address. I don't like bothering Mr Smith.'

'Is that Ambrose Smith?'

She nodded. 'He was her lawyer for many years.'

'I know of him; he was my uncle's lawyer too,' John said, and as if that created an affinity between them the girl relaxed and smiled so John didn't tell her that he'd never met the man.

'You got everything else—the proceeds of the sale of the house?'

Again she nodded. 'He sent me a cheque.' She smiled again. 'I didn't need to come at all—it wasn't just because of the painting—but now I could afford the trip and I wanted to look at the house again, even if someone else owns it. But the painting is special. It was a family portrait, done from photographs of relatives in Poland and my father was in it . . .'

He took notes. 'You mentioned other things.'

'Some jewellery, nothing very valuable, but I would like to have what belonged to Lucy.' She had no definite description of those items apart from 'rings and brooches'.

'Right,' he said. 'I'll get in touch with Mr Smith for other details but I'll need your address. How long are you staying?' The coffee arrived, not in the usual mugs but in cups and saucers, and John was impressed.

'I'm not sure,' she said shyly, giving a strong impression of someone who had inherited money and was not sure how much she should spend. 'In Edinburgh for a bit and then I think I'll see something of Scotland, maybe for a week or so.'

And for the next half-hour they discussed the essential tourist areas. He liked her but guessed that she was very immature for her years and that this trip was a big adventure.

After she'd gone he gave Tollis the details. 'What do you do if the lawyer doesn't have a forwarding address for the housekeeper?'

Tollis shrugged. 'She won't necessarily have stolen the stuff but may not have wanted to lug a painting with her into retirement. She'll have told someone where she was going, or neighbours will know of relatives—it's just a case of checking them out. Most likely she'll still be in Edinburgh—I just hope she didn't dump the painting in a sale room before she took off. It won't be worth much, except to Maria. Didn't you say you had an appointment with Smith about Rees's will?'

'That's right. I'll ask him if he has Mrs Pearson's address and I'll follow it up if you like.'

Tollis grinned and handed the brief notes back to John. 'An excuse to stay out of the office for a bit.'

'What's he like? Rees mentioned him occasionally but I never met him.'

Tollis reached for a cigarette, found the packet was empty and tossed it towards an overflowing bin, missed, and it landed among the rest of the screwed up papers on the floor. 'Family lawyer, rather than the conveyancing sort, paternal so I hear.' He opened a new packet of cigarettes. 'Very successful if his standard of living is anything to go by. Rees stuck with him for years. He'll have the woman's address and that will save us some leg work and keep the expense down at the same time.'

'So it's routine, then,' John said, disappointed.

Tollis nodded. 'Afraid so,' he said, already dismissing the Maria Twarog inquiry as of minor interest.

CHAPTER 2

John left Kramer House just after 6.30 that evening and headed for Clare Aitken's flat, knowing that Tollis thought it was odd that two people who were in love should want to live apart.

It was one of the evenings when she stayed late at her office so he defrosted a couple of steaks in the microwave, peppered them ready for the grill and prepared a salad. When she arrived he was watching the news, sprawled in a chair by the gas fire with a glass of wine in his hand.

'Pour me one—how did the funeral go?' She pulled off scarf and coat and bent to put her cold hands inside the collar of his shirt, drew his face forward so that she could kiss him with cold lips. He set down his glass and pulled her on to his lap and then wrapped his arms around her body. He heard her sigh as she snuggled close as if to draw warmth from him and he felt her dark silky hair against his neck.

'It was bleak. I'm glad I didn't let you come,' he murmured with his lips close to the top of her head.

'Poor Rees. I never got to know him and I know he didn't have many friends, but to shut people out of his funeral . . .'

She looked up at John as if to gauge how he was feeling but the truth was that he didn't know himself. He bent to kiss her lightly.

'No one got close to Rees and he didn't like sentiment. The thought of people crying over him would have horrified him,' he said. Then he pushed her off his knee and got up himself. 'Get changed and I'll cook your supper.'

The kitchen was as large and square as all the rooms in the old Georgian house that had been split into flats many years before. Clare had modernized the kitchen as far as it was possible, with units on three walls and a round dining table near the fourth, but it meant there was a lot of walking to and fro as a meal was prepared. Clare appeared before the steaks were ready and began to set the table. It would have been a very domestic scene if she hadn't decided to slip into a thin top and tight ski pants with nothing underneath. The material revealed curves that were unfettered and completely distracted his attention.

'You'll burn the steaks,' she murmured, as usual fully aware of his thoughts. She pushed back her shoulder-length dark hair with a familiar gesture and it was almost her undoing. He reached for her but she dodged away and picked up the bowl of salad and it ended up as a barrier between their bodies.

'Witch.'

'I'm hungry.'

They ate in front of the fire with one of Clare's CDs playing in the background; a moody piece that competed with the sounds of the wind and the tree branches scratching against the window. It was a night to be inside, to know that very soon he would have Clare's body close to his in bed. That was why it was easy to spend this in-between time telling her about the problems at Kramer's and wondering how the hell he was going to run such a large business and still make a profit. He also told her about Val.

'Knowing my uncle, he must have had a great deal of faith in her ability because usually he was never comfortable with women.'

'Maybe you read him wrong—he probably felt safer,' she commented. 'You told me he didn't make friends easily but to a man like that a woman is no threat. I suspect he used her as a tool.'

And she was right, of course. 'Then it really is a wait and

see game.' Her body was warm under his hand, her skin
fragrant. 'Let's go to bed,' he said, and Clare pretended to
consider, smiled and seemed about to agree, when the
phone rang and she held it out to him.

'Tollis,' she said, twisting her mouth ruefully.

'There have been break-ins at Kramer properties. I've
had Chief Inspector Jamieson on the phone. Sorry if I interrupted anything.'

John looked over at Clare, her face flushed pink and
glowing from the heat of the fire and the long lines of her
body relaxed. He cleared his throat and forced his attention
back to Tollis. 'How do you mean, Kramer properties?'

'Sentinel looks after the security of the buildings that
Kramer manages—that you rent out among other things.
Our policeman friend thinks you should be on the scene.'

'When?'

'I said I'd get in touch with you and he'd meet us here
—he's on his way now,' Tollis said regretfully, as if he could
picture the scene he was asking John to leave.

'OK. I'll be right there.' He replaced the receiver and
shrugged.

'It shouldn't take long and then I'll be back,' he told a
curious Clare. 'Something about break-ins . . . I'd better
put in an appearance.'

'Huh. I'll leave the dishes for you to wash,' she breathed
as he bent to kiss her. 'And if you're late don't wake me
up.'

He cursed Jamieson as he fastened the seat-belt of the
Granada, Rees's car. Usually he drove a car from the
Kramer pool but there was no point in letting the Granada
sit idle. Hopefully the meeting with Jamieson wouldn't take
that long, he thought, but was to be proved wrong.
Jamieson had arrived at Sentinel before him and was drinking some of Tollis's vile coffee, but he made it clear that he
wanted both of them to visit the scenes of the crimes.

'There's something very wrong,' he said cryptically.

Mike Cairns, one of Tollis's older employees, slipped into
the room at that point and Jamieson, who knew Mike and

a lot of the other regular employees by sight, paused while Mike took a seat. 'There have been other similar break-ins around Edinburgh—not just yours, and it's looking like the start of an epidemic. They were all done very recently, by non-professionals, quick jobs that were crude in-and-out affairs. A case of grab what you can but with no preliminary scouting as far as we could see. The Kramer ones are different from the rest.'

'In what way?' Tollis was leaning forward, his eyes intent and serious.

'They had plenty of time, for one thing, because they knew how to deal with the alarms.'

'Do you think the same people are doing them all?' Tollis wanted to know, but Jamieson shrugged.

'Could be, but in your case they just walked in—I smell an inside job.'

Tollis was nodding and he looked worried. John had been silent but now he wanted an explanation.

'I don't understand much of this. These are houses standing empty that Kramer's are trying to rent out for the legal owners?'

Tollis nodded. 'When owners go abroad, or for whatever reason their home is going to be empty, they either want an income to cover the mortgage—in which case your property management department finds reputable tenants—or they want someone looking after it while it's empty. Sentinel is responsible for all aspects of the security of the building as well as the maintenance, right down to checking that there are no burst pipes—that sort of thing. That applies if the property is tenanted—rent collection—or if it stands empty. The Inspector is suggesting that someone in the company is giving out addresses and details of the alarm systems.'

John groaned and slid further down in his chair. 'And I'll have to find out how many have access to that sort of information.'

'And there are my men. No, I don't think it came from here but I'll still have to check it out,' Tollis said with a glance at the policeman. So far Mike Cairns had said nothing but he was a dour man at the best of times. Now Tollis looked across at him but Mike's beefy face was impassive.

'Right.' Jamieson, the smallest man in the room at just under six feet, got up from his seat with a briskness that none of the rest of them felt. 'Now that you know my thoughts on the matter we'll go and take a look. You'll want to report to your clients anyway, I expect. Do you have inventories of the contents?'

'They'll be with John's staff,' Tollis said and John gave a small shrug.

'I can't do anything about that until the morning.'

Jamieson wouldn't accept that. 'There must be someone you can call out. The sooner we know what is missing . . .'

John asked for the addresses of the houses and then phoned Val who listened without interrupting.

'I know what you want. I'll meet you at the first one as quickly as I can.'

It turned out to be a long night. The first house they visited was on Corstorphine hill with a view of the River Forth, but set so far back and up from the road that it was hard to understand how any criminal would know it was there. Surrounded by trees, the house was now ablaze with lights and two police cars were parked in the front drive.

'There's not much mess,' Jamieson said as they went in by the front door.

The layout of the house reminded John of Elmwood but it was more richly furnished. The owners had obviously travelled a lot and brought back souvenirs; expensive rugs and ornaments of jade and ivory. The thieves had apparently not been interested in those but it wasn't until Val arrived with the lists that they could begin to check what was gone.

'Leave my men to do this—I don't want anyone else handling things,' the policeman said. 'My guess is that it will be mainly the smaller stuff that's easy to get rid of— looks like some miniatures are gone from over there . . .' and he pointed to the marks left on the wallpaper. He shrugged. 'We know where to start looking and if they're local we'll get them eventually.'

Tollis was nodding as if he understood all that, but Jamieson explained for John's sake. 'Most thieves don't know what to take, so they go for what looks good—the shiny things like silver and jewellery. I've known them take plate and paste and cheap carriage clocks and leave Old Masters on the wall. Just sometimes they have someone backing them, providing them with a shopping list of what to look for, but your lists don't state the values, thank goodness. Once we know what's gone, we'll know who we're looking for—pros or amateurs.'

Tollis had disappeared to check the alarm system and he came back shaking his head. 'Looks as if you're right, they knew how to shut things off. I'll have somebody's head for this.' His mouth shut in a grim line and John knew that it was because Sentinel's reputation was at stake. 'Where next?' Tollis went on, and Jamieson gave an address in the Barnton district.

They found much the same thing there, but by now the neighbours had heard what had happened and they were out in their gardens watching the police activity, despite the cold wind that was now so strong that it tugged at their coats and stung their cheeks as the watchers stood in uneasy groups. No doubt, John thought, they were saying, 'It could have been us.'

'I know this house,' Mike Cairns said suddenly. It was the first time he'd spoken and they all turned to look at him. 'It's one that I've checked out myself and there's a safe.'

'Christ, not that too,' Tollis muttered.

'Let's go see,' Jamieson grunted.

'How did you know about all this?' Tollis asked. 'If the alarms didn't go off . . .'

Jamieson frowned before answering. 'Anonymous call from a woman who gave us the addresses. Haven't figured that out yet, but it happens. Could have been spite, or a battered wife hoping we'd lock hubby up for a year or two.'

Mike led them to the master bedroom and pulled back a rug near the window. Beneath it was a steel plate with a combination lock set into its surface but it looked untouched.

'Thank God for that,' Tollis breathed. 'Do we know what's inside?' Val looked at her list and shook her head. 'Unspecified,' she said quietly. 'But we have the combination.'

Tollis groaned and Jamieson reached for the paper that Val held. 'We'll open it after it's been checked for prints,' he commented drily.

They didn't need to see any more, so they left Jamieson poking about at the Barnton scene and drove back to Kramer House. Tollis kept no regular working hours and didn't see anything wrong with holding a conference at two in the morning and since it was too late to disturb Clare anyway, John agreed that it was necessary. Val left them to it and went home.

'We have two choices,' Tollis said bluntly. 'We move in openly to see who has access to the information, interview each member of staff, check to see if anyone is spending new money, etcetera, thereby tipping him off that we know what's going on, or we do it clandestinely which will take longer.'

'Val will know who has access and if there are only a few I vote for a quiet investigation,' John said instantly. 'There's already an unsettled feeling and I've got enough on my plate.'

Tollis agreed, but John got the feeling that he would have preferred the other method for the sake of speed.

'Tell her to look out for absentees. Jamieson said a woman phoned, and it could be a member of staff having second thoughts, in which case she may be scared to show her face. Then you can start to tighten up your system.'

'What if it's in your department? Your men have all the answers, the layout of the houses, the alarms . . .'

Tollis looked down at his hands and then across at Mike. The two men seemed to communicate without the need to speak and now both looked grim. 'I've thought of that. Tomorrow there will be no quiet investigation here, I promise you.' He paused to light a cigarette and drew the first of the smoke deep into his lungs. 'There's something else to think about. If there's a leak, the culprit may have handed over a complete list of properties—and I mean the lot, even the occupied ones. All they have to do is pick and choose their targets and that means anywhere in Edinburgh. I don't have enough men to cover them all. There's no way we can watch all the houses, so we have to expect Jamieson to report more cases.'

And as if Jamieson had heard him, the phone rang and Tollis's face told its own story. When he hung up he looked furious.

'Two more have been reported since we left. They're on the loose tonight and God knows how many more they'll turn over.'

They chewed over possible action for another hour but the plain facts were that there wasn't much they could do in the short term and John went up to the top floor flat which he and Rees had often used, feeling utterly depressed with the whole Kramer business.

He didn't sleep well and at six was up and dressed in running gear. The city was quiet as he jogged down the High Street to the bottom of the Royal Mile and on to the grassy area at the foot of Arthur's Seat. The route was one that he ran whenever he had the time because it was the nearest area of greenery, not because it was historic. He was not conscious of his surroundings for most of the time and after the initial shock of the early morning frost he forgot the cold. The purpose of the run was to let his feet take over the rhythm and then he could concentrate on the problem of what to do with his inheritance, Kramer Property.

His breathing grew ragged as he negotiated a hilly track and several times his feet slipped on the frost-rimed grass, but once through the usual pain barrier he picked up speed and pushed himself hard. Kramer's. His brain spelled it out one letter at a time but even on the slithering downward run he hadn't found a solution. The only thing he did consider was to ask the solicitor, Ambrose Smith, for advice when he saw him later that morning.

He finished the punishing run by taking the stairs in Kramer House instead of using the lift and as he passed through the Sentinel Agency's floor he saw that it was lit. Tollis had either arrived early or he'd once more spent the night in the building, sleeping on the small bunk in the back room. John was tempted to join him for breakfast but in the end went up to the flat to shower and change and when he went into the Kramer offices he found that Val had arrived early.

'I want to make a start on checking who has access to the lists. I can do some of it here but I may have to go down to the property management section.' She sounded reluctant to do that and he knew why. The department was in a high and narrow building in the Canongate. Only fifty yards separated it from Kramer House but because it was set apart it had developed an autonomy of its own. Rees had left it well alone because there was a lot of hassle in playing janitor to properties, and he'd given the staff a more or less free hand. At one time he'd considered getting shot of that side of the business but it had survived purely because it made a profit.

'I've only been there a couple of times,' he said. 'It's a maze of small rooms and it's overcrowded.'

'Exactly,' she said drily. Then as if that needed an explanation she went on. 'I did mention to Mr Kramer that the whole business is too disjointed, with bits spread all over the place, but he didn't see the need to change things.' And he guessed that Val was more frustrated than she let on.

'It's something we could talk about when I get a meeting set up,' he said and her face brightened. 'But not now. I've got an appointment.' He walked down to the West End to see the solicitor because his premises were just off Princes Street where parking was impossible. The sun had come out and showed the view of the city, from the height of the

Mound, at its best, apart from the tapering Scott monument that towered over all the other buildings. Stone-cleaning was in progress and for some time it had been cloaked in scaffolding and plastic sheets—he smiled as he remembered Tollis's crude comments that it looked like a gigantic phallic symbol wearing a condom.

He was five minutes early as he climbed the steps to the lawyer's office where a shining brass plate said Ambrose Smith, Writer to the Signet.

The receptionist was fortyish and pleasant.

'Go right in,' she said in a smooth tone that might have been cultivated to match the deep carpets and antique furniture. The opulence was there but it was not ostentatious, just a pointer to the man's clients that this was a successful solicitor's place of business. Smith himself was everyone's idea of a legal man, tall and lean and serious. His sparse greying hair was carefully combed, his suit well cut and his fingers surprisingly cold considering the warmth of the room.

'Your uncle's death was a shock,' he said, still holding on to John's hand in a firm grasp. 'I would have attended the funeral, but respected his wishes.'

John hoped that he wasn't going to go down memory lane. He wasn't. Smith got right down to business and, as expected, the will contained no surprises. Rees had left shares and a lump sum to Gwen, although the business came to him, and a trust had been set up for David as well as Janet's pension. The lawyer had put on half-moon glasses and each time he paused in his reading he removed them and used them to emphasize a point, but his tone never varied. He gave the details of the considerable inheritance as if he handled such estates on a regular basis.

'The business of executry will take some time and there's a lot of gathering together to be done before I apply for confirmation. In the meantime, I'm here whenever you need any advice.'

How he would enjoy that, John thought. What Smith was actually saying was that he would somehow find the time in his busy schedule to advise this green young man in the intricacies of business. It brought on a wave of intense dislike and yet he had no grounds at all for such a feeling. It was what Tollis called his gut reaction, totally instinctive. He studied Smith as he talked; his gestures and expressions all seemed practised, and why not? He had a professional approach, a face that he showed clients, and very likely it had become second nature. Maybe he was quite different with his friends, had charm of a sort, but John found it all off-putting, like speaking to someone through a glass screen in a bank.

'Thanks, I'll keep it in mind.' He was anxious to leave now that he'd lost his inclination to discuss Kramer business with Smith, but he still had to ask questions on behalf of Tollis.

'There is one other thing. I'm trying to help one of Tollis's clients, a Canadian girl called Maria Twarog.' He noted the sudden spark in the lawyer's eyes and guessed that he remembered the girl.

'She wants to trace her aunt's housekeeper who was holding on to some small items for her. The woman's moved on and there's no forwarding address.'

Smith pursed his lips in deep thought, then spoke into an intercom.

'Look out the Simpson file, please.' He drummed slender fingers on the desk. 'I'm surprised that she didn't get in touch with me. How did she come to write to your firm?'

'She approached the Sentinel Agency—Tollis was Rees's partner at one time, as you know—but she didn't write, she's here.'

The lawyer blinked and put on the glasses again. They magnified his eyes and John felt as if he was a speck of dust under a microscope.

'Here? Then she should have come to me.' The fingers drummed again but faster now. 'There's no need for her to pay good money to a detective agency; tell her I'll see that she gets her . . . items.'

John smothered a smile of amusement. No wonder the

man was successful if he resented a small fee slipping away.
'Tollis says it's a routine thing so the fee won't be very
much.'

'That's not the point. It's unfinished business and I don't
see the need . . .' The secretary brought in a slim folder
and the lawyer glanced through it. 'I don't seem to have a
forwarding address either, but tell the young lady I'll get it
for her.'

John was getting irritated. 'How? Tollis is used to tracing
people.' He stood up. 'Leave it with us.' He moved towards
the door but Smith was still displeased and unwilling to let
it go.

'Do you know where she is staying in Edinburgh? I feel
I should get in touch with her at least,' he said.

'I don't have the address with me,' John replied. 'But I'll
let her know you're anxious to help.'

He was glad to get outside. Smith had followed him to
the front door and stood there as John walked away, which
gave him a queasy feeling in his stomach. How money-
grabbing could you get? And as he told Tollis later, 'What
a fuss about nothing, he's a leech. I'm not letting him
handle any of our business in the future.'

'Maybe he's successful because he takes good care of his
clients' money—it's become a habit to count the pennies.
Rees never complained.'

'I didn't like him.'

'You're doing it again,' Tollis said with a grin. 'Playing
hunches—what gets your suspicious hackles up?'

'OK, so I don't really know the man,' John admitted
'but I don't have to, do I?'

'No, and if you feel like that why don't you seek out the
housekeeper—get there before him?'

That appealed to John. 'You're on. Tell me where to
start.'

'There's just one thing—you'll be on your own as far as
leg-work is concerned. I have to put a cost on every job and
finding Mrs Pearson doesn't justify a lot of expense.'

For once Tollis was to be proved wrong. Locating Lucy

Simpson's ex-housekeeper was to be very expensive indeed, for a lot of people.

CHAPTER 3

Val had noted the names of those members of staff who had direct access to the lists of vacant properties but she wasn't sure it would be helpful.

'There's a 'flu epidemic and some are off sick. And I haven't even included the surveyors who might know the details. In theory, almost anyone could look up the information and we'll have to find some other way of handling this.'

'Mm. Then we'll have to tighten up the procedure and hope that the police catch the villains in the act.'

'Will they want these names?'

John shook his head. 'I won't put people under suspicion unless there's a definite pointer that they're involved. We'll wait.'

He spent the rest of the morning working with Val and discovering that she was a good teacher. He noticed too that she was wearing a bright blouse in a mixture of rust and orange shades that gave her pale complexion a glow; she no longer melted into the background as she had done when Rees was around.

'I won't be around this afternoon but you can get my whereabouts from Tollis if you need me,' he told her. 'And tomorrow may be the same.'

He asked if she could manage, was certain she could, and her quiet nod confirmed that. 'And I think we should arrange a meeting of the senior staff for next week.'

'You've decided what you're going to do, then?'

'Mm.' He didn't give her any clues to his plans because they were sketchy anyway, and got ready for a pub lunch with Tollis. Val left for an extended lunch break so it was

her deputy who came to tell him that there was a call for
him.
'That young woman who called before. You said . . .'
'Put her through.' He dropped his coat on a chair and
picked up his extension.
'This is John Leith,' he said.
There was silence for a while and he wondered if she was
there and then he heard her indrawn breath. When she
spoke it was so quietly that he could barely hear her.
'Mr Leith, can I talk to you—somewhere away from
your office?' Her voice was high-pitched and sounded very
young.
'Can you tell me what it's about? And your name?'
'Bridie McGuire.' The words came out in a whisper of
breath and he knew that she was crying. He sat down and
waited for her to speak again, but by now she was sobbing
and he couldn't understand what she was saying.
'Bridie,' he interrupted. 'I'm free in an hour's time. Do
you know the Italian place around the corner from the
office? I'll wait there for you. You will come?'
'Yes. If I can.'
'Can't you tell me now?' he asked gently, afraid that after
she hung up the phone she would get cold feet again.
'I don't know where to start . . .'
'Then we'll meet and you can take your time. I'll be there
in one hour.'
'All right.'
He sat there for some time, just thinking, then went to
Val's room and looked through the lists on her desk. Half
way down one page he saw the name Bridie McGuire. So
she was one of his employees and beside her name Val had
pencilled in 'on sick list'. He took a note of her address and
put the slip of paper in his pocket, just in case the girl did
get cold feet and failed to turn up.
Tollis made a guess as to why the girl sounded frightened.
'Someone used her for information and she's having second
thoughts—that ties in with the woman who phoned the
police. It must have been her. At least that solves our

problem and I'm glad the news didn't leak from Sentinel.'

John remembered the desperation in the girl's voice and couldn't share his relief. 'I was going to look for that house-keeper this afternoon but I'll see this girl first.'

Tollis was looking amused. The big man had chosen the corner seat in the pub, a long green padded bench that was substantial enough to bear his weight, and now he leaned back to look at John with a twitching smile on his lips. 'There isn't enough upstairs to keep you busy?'

'Plenty. But I'm letting it simmer for a week. Anyway, Bridie McGuire *is* Kramer business.'

'Sure she is, and a good excuse to sniff around. Let me know how it develops.'

John waited for over half an hour in the Italian café, sitting in the window seat so that he could watch for her, but she didn't appear and there was no hesitant girl out in the street either. He wasn't really surprised. In the end he walked around the back of the Kramer building to where he'd parked his car and set off for the address he'd taken from the list. It turned out to be in a tenement building and it was the girl's mother who answered the door.

'Bridie doesn't live here any more,' the woman said, hold-ing the door so that he couldn't see beyond her.

'Oh. Then can you give me her new address?'

The woman looked him over as if assessing who he might be, so John explained. 'My name is John Leith and Bridie works for me,' he said quietly. 'She has been off work and I came to see how she was.'

The woman looked sceptical but she stood aside and asked him in. The flat was very tidy but was gloomy because it faced another tall building that shut out the light. He sat on a settee and the tired-looking woman sat on a chair facing him.

'Bridie didn't tell the office that she'd moved,' he said.

'She hardly told me,' her mother said drily. 'She just said she was going and that was that.' Then with a mixture of anger and anxiety the words came tumbling out. 'She's always been a quiet girl, no problem, always giving me money from her wages without a word of protest. We managed, just. Now . . .' She tailed off, shaking her head. 'Suddenly she's got the money to move out and run a car.' She sounded almost resentful.

'When did all this start?'

'A couple of weeks back, not all that long.' The woman looked down at her clasped hands. 'I worry about her. She's not the sort of girl to know about men . . .'

'There is a man involved, then?'

She shrugged. 'There has to be, but she won't say. When I tried to find out she told me to mind my own business— quite snappy, she was. So if she's sick I don't know about it, and I don't have her address,' the woman said with tight lips. 'My own daughter moved out and I don't even know where she went. And I don't know how much longer I can last without her money coming in.' Worry lines formed around her eyes but they weren't all for her financial situation.

'She's not a pretty girl, Mr Leith. She's quiet and naïve and something has gone to her head and no good will come of it.'

She closed the door firmly behind him when he left and he knew she probably spent lonely hours in her tidy flat, wondering where her lost daughter was and if she would come home.

It seemed logical to go next to the department where Bridie worked, so he drove back towards the property management building. The girls at the reception desk recognized him and when he explained that he wanted to speak to someone who worked with Bridie, they directed him to the first floor.

'She's left home,' he told the two girls who sat in front of computers. 'Has she been talking about her plans, where she is living now?'

Both girls exchanged a glance and then shook their heads. From their expressions John guessed that they didn't much care.

'What sort of girl is she?' he asked. There was no answer.

'Oh, come on, she sat here with you all day—she must have said something.'

'She was very quiet,' one said. 'She never had much to say and she didn't seem to do anything—she never went out.'

The other girl spoke. 'She stayed in at night, with her mother.'

'What difference does that make?'

A shrug. 'She was weird, didn't talk about films or the telly. Her clothes were . . . old-fashioned.' She giggled and the other girl joined in, but both were nervous about telling the boss anything. John tried to keep his temper, pulled up a chair and sat down facing them.

'Look, the girl is in some sort of trouble and I need to find her.'

Instant interest.

'What sort of trouble?' one asked, and he could imagine the gossip that would circulate around the office.

'She's ill,' he said flatly. 'Do you know where she moved to?'

'She's been different lately,' one of them said sulkily. 'She got new clothes and a car and kept on about moving in with her new boyfriend, making it into a big mystery. It was all rubbish. Nobody liked her before, and after that they couldn't stand her. She didn't tell us where her new flat was.'

'I see,' he said, replacing the chair and leaving the two of them to speculate why the boss should be interested in someone like Bridie McGuire. He gave up on that inquiry and drove to the street where Maria Twarog's Aunt Lucy had lived, to look for the other missing woman.

It was a new experience to knock on doors and he discovered how it felt to be a salesman. The first woman who answered his ring stuck her head around the door suspiciously.

'I don't buy anything at the door,' she said, beginning to close it in his face.

'I'm making inquiries about a missing person,' he said

and that got her attention. 'The housekeeper at No. 6—
Mrs Pearson—do you have any idea where she went when
the house was sold?'

'Is it sold? No one's moved in.'

He followed her glance across the street to where the
garden looked overgrown and neglected and where he could
just see through the trees that the windows were curtainless.

'Maybe they're not ready to move in. Do you know if she
went to stay with relatives? Did she mention any plans?'

The woman pondered, then shook her head. 'I didn't
know her all that well. You could try No. 8 but they're out
all day. She used to go in there to do some cleaning for
them.'

'Thanks, I'll come back later, then,' he said, and he left
the woman openly curious.

'I'm no good at this,' he told Tollis later. 'A whole afternoon and I've achieved nothing.'

'Routine is boring. Costly in time and petrol,' Tollis said,
leaning far back in his chair so that his feet could rest on his
desk. 'The girl will phone again if she's desperate enough
and you can go to No. 8 this evening and see the neighbours
about the housekeeper.'

'This evening I might take Clare out to make up for last
night.'

'Gwen phoned, by the way. You've to phone David's
school about camping equipment, or something.'

John hauled himself up out of his chair. 'I'd better go
and do that now. He's going away for the Easter holiday.'

He sat in Rees's office—he still couldn't think of it as his
yet—and was about to dial the school number when Val
came in to say there was a personal call for him.

'A man—wouldn't give his name.'

'Put him though,' he said resignedly, then reached for
the phone.

'John Leith,' he announced. His mind was on where he
could take Clare that was different from their usual haunts,
so he was quite unprepared for the rasping anger in the

man's voice. He jerked up in the chair as soon as the tirade began.

'Keep your nose out of things that don't concern you—you hear me?'

'Who are you?'

There was a short pause during which he heard traffic sounds in the background. Then the man began again but the tone was more controlled and menacing. 'That's just it—you don't know me but I know you. I heard you were poking around, asking questions—and it's none of your bloody affair. I'm going to be watching you and you'd better drop this inquiry or you'll be very sorry. Know what I mean?'

He didn't wait for an answer, but hung up, and John was left with a lot of unanswered questions.

Poking around, asking questions—Bridie's boyfriend didn't like that.

He phoned David's school and arranged to see the warden on Saturday to get a list of the things that his son still needed for the camping trip.

'And I'd like to take him out for the afternoon.'

Then he phoned Gwen and was told that they still had some work to do in clearing out Rees's things.

'There are some bits and pieces that you should decide about but Janet is leaving them aside. I think it helps her to keep busy . . .'

'There's no rush.' His mind was only partly on what his sister was saying and partly on the man's anger . . . the implicit warning . . .

'Are you all right, John? You sound tired,' Gwen said.

'I'm fine. What time is your plane on Friday? I could come down and look over Rees's stuff and then drive you to Turnhouse.'

'I can easily take a taxi.'

He arranged to be at Elmwood for lunch and then bring her back with him. His duty calls done, he thought over what the man had said. Bridie McGuire had been persuaded to hand over lists of empty properties to an unknown person—probably this caller—and now she was regretting it. She had not gone home and the man didn't want anyone interfering in his profitable scam, so he was issuing threats. Whether or not he meant to use violence to protect himself was another matter. It didn't seem very likely. John pushed the whole business out of his mind and phoned Clare at her office.

'How about eating out tonight?'

'I think I'd rather have a quiet supper at home. It's been one of those days,' she sighed.

'Hasn't it just,' he replied.

'John?' Her telepathic instincts were at work but he was quick to reassure her.

'Just hassle—see you this evening.'

'And no interruptions this time?'

'Promise.'

Then he went downstairs to tell Tollis about the phone call. He remembered the exact words and Tollis listened intently. 'So he's warning you off. Did he sound the sort to use force?'

'He just sounded angry, but you could say the threat of violence was there.'

'So what are you going to do?'

'I'm going to look for Bridie. He might get rough with her too if I don't convince her to go back home.'

'Well, you know the ropes, take extra care and don't linger on dark streets. What was his voice like?'

'He was no ordinary tough—he sounded educated. Local accent but not a strong one. Like you, in fact, and mature. Hardly the type to be attracted to the Bridie I've been hearing about. Her mother and the girls who work with her describe her as being plain, old-fashioned, unpopular—she doesn't seem to have anything going for her.'

'Just the type our friend was looking for, in fact. A girl like that would be highly flattered by any sort of attention —he wouldn't have much difficulty persuading her. She was ripe for the picking, as they say.'

'And now she's got cold feet.'

'And that could mean trouble for her. I think we should let Jamieson know.'

John was relieved that Tollis had come to the same conclusion as he had. He'd never met Bridie and had no reason to feel sorry for her, but he couldn't forget how she'd sounded on the phone.

The policeman said a photograph of the girl would be helpful, but after inquiries in the office where she worked it was no surprise to John to learn that no one had ever taken a snap of her. 'She never came to the office parties,' was the excuse.

'I'll call on her mother again before I got back to No. 8 to ask about the housekeeper,' he told Tollis. 'Then I'll be at Clare's flat.'

'I'll try not to interrupt this time,' Tollis replied. He was teasing, but there was a hint of wistfulness or envy in his voice that made John wonder about Tollis's love-life. He knew there had been a wife at some time and that the marriage had ended in divorce, but no one would ever know more. In fact, John had never heard him called by his first name and he wondered if anyone knew it apart from Rees. In a way, he thought as he left the building, Tollis had a lot of Rees's qualities; both had the need to keep their own thoughts and lives private. It must come from their time together in the intelligence service, but in Tollis's case there was no narrow-mindedness, no tight control of emotions.

Bridie's mother seemed quite welcoming this time and he guessed that she got few visitors. 'Yes, of course I have photographs but not very recent ones.' She fetched albums and flicked through the pages of baby snaps which showed that Bridie had not even been a pretty baby. Her features were flat, the complexion pasty, the eyes dull. Later snaps showed that the schoolgirl hadn't improved much.

'Why do you want one?' her mother suddenly asked and it caught John unawares. He explained that he'd mentioned Bridie to friend who knew how to trace people. 'We need to ask her something about her job—to satisfy clients,' he said hurriedly. It sounded weak but the woman was curiously pleased with the explanation. Proud even, and that made him uncomfortable with the near lie.

'It must be unusual these days for employers to care,' she said and that made him feel worse. In the end the best photograph was a blurred image of an overweight girl of twenty but it was the most recent one she had.

'You'll tell her that I'm worried and I wish she'd come home,' she said as he left.

He'd had a sniff of the seamier side of detective work but he hadn't expected to have to resort to lies. He didn't like to think of how the mother would react if the girl was charged with complicity in theft. No wonder Tollis and the others who worked for Sentinel had developed a cynical attitude, he reflected as he drove to his next call. They had probably seen it all and were no longer surprised by anything, like Chief Inspector Jamieson who had the same tired look of acceptance.

A professional couple called Brodie lived at No. 8 and they were having a pre-dinner drink when he arrived at their door. Their living-room had the stale air of being unused all day while they were at work, and was slightly dusty now that their helper from next door was no longer around.

'It's so hard to find a part-time cleaner who is reliable,' the woman said. 'Mrs Pearson was a gem.'

'Do you know where she went?'

They looked at each other with the equality that comes from both contributing similar salaries to the joint income and it occurred to him that women developed a new bearing when they held responsible jobs. Like Val. Like Clare.

'The old lady left her some money but I don't think it was enough to retire on,' Mrs Brodie said before throwing a question at her husband. 'Didn't she mention a sister here in town?'

He shrugged, as if cleaning ladies were out of his sphere. Mrs Brodie was keen to help, but although she tried hard, she couldn't remember much.

'I seem to remember that Mrs Pearson's brother died and she was going to live with his widow for a bit, to keep her company. I only saw her briefly, you see,' she said regretfully.

'Is there anyone else who might know?'

'We don't know the neighbours—you don't when you work full time. Why not try the little shop at the end of the street?'

It was closed, of course. He tried a few more houses, battled against the salesman image, got nowhere. People didn't get friendly any more; they were too busy with their own affairs, watched television, never saw the vandalism that could happen across the street, didn't get to know their neighbours. Mrs Pearson hadn't registered on anyone. He gave up and headed for Clare's flat, pondering on Tollis's comment that it would be an easy matter—routine—to trace the housekeeper who had taken charge of one painting and some odds and ends of jewellery.

Clare was interested and thought over the problem as they ate supper.

'Why not write to her?' she said, and when he pointed out that he had nowhere to send it she dug her finger in his ribs. 'She might be getting her mail re-directed, though.'

'Not for as long as this. Lucy Simpson died some time last year.'

He thought about it, though, and it wasn't such a daft idea. 'The post office might have a record of the re-directed mail. Of course I would have thought of it myself eventually,' he said.

'Huh.'

'OK, so I'll reward you later.'

She set down her coffee cup and all the laughter slowly disappeared from her eyes to be replaced by a look that he knew well. 'How much later?' she said softly.

'Like right now.'

They undressed without haste in the bedroom. Clare moved around with her back to him and as always his eyes were drawn to the exit scar of the bullet wound on her shoulder. The scar would fade in time, the doctor had told him, but that didn't make it any easier for him to forgive the man who'd pulled the trigger. The doctor, who had previously worked in Glasgow, had seen many such injuries and had developed a special interest in the subject. When John asked the obvious questions, he got far more detail than he wanted, but he had taken it all in. For some macabre reason it had helped to feed his anger at the man who had so easily inflicted the wound, and he'd needed to sustain the anger at the time. A psychologist might see it differently, but it all boiled down to the need to hate the man with the gun. Every word was still imprinted on his mind, even if it had sounded like a pathology report.

'A bullet, you see, revolves at almost three thousand times a second and it wipes all its surface dirt on the skin, like using it as a doormat, and it sort of wags its tail end as it goes into the body.'

The body. The doctor even illustrated what he meant with gestures from a wagging finger. John had waited grimly for the rest.

'The entrance wound is a small round hole, unlike the exit wound where bone splinters and the wobbling momentum of the bullet have torn the flesh.' He had spread his fingers wider. Then he seemed to realize what he was saying and who he was saying it to. 'But she was lucky, there is no major damage. And she's young and healthy.'

Torn Clare's flesh. The horror came back.

Clare turned and saw his expression, read his mind; her hand went up to touch the small round area of puckered flesh above her breast. She didn't like to remember the events of that night, so he said nothing. The man whose finger had pulled the trigger was dead. It was over and done with, but deep down he knew that the possibility of exposing her to danger once more was making him hesitate about working permanently with Tollis. It was unlikely that there would be another man who would not think twice about turning a gun on a woman, but lightning had been known to strike more than once at the same target.

Clare was already under the duvet. 'I'm cold. Come to bed.'

So he slid in beside her and felt her chilled flesh against his own and the mechanics of love-making, the discoveries of new pleasures, drove the morbid thoughts of violence far from his mind, for one more night.

He stopped off at the Sentinel floor the next morning and caught Tollis in the act of shaving. 'Don't you ever go home?'

'Doesn't seem worth it. Was Mike around when you came in?'

John perched on a bare spot on the desk. 'Funny you should say that. I saw his car near Clare's flat last night— he drove by as I went in her gate. But I've not seen him this morning.'

Tollis patted on aftershave and rubbed the remnants over his short dark hair. His shirt was crisply fresh, his pants pressed and John watched with amusement as he rummaged for a tie in his desk drawer.

'Going somewhere special?'

'Your friend and mine, solicitor Smith, is coming over. You forgot to mention he wanted Maria's address.'

'Why come here in person? You could have told him that on the phone.'

'Says he'd like to see the set-up here—just out of interest —before he visits you for some signatures on documents. And would I like to look out the young lady's address so that he can deal with her little bit of business? He can go stand in front of the one o'clock gun up at the Castle!'

'You're not giving him her address?'

'She's *my* client.'

Tollis slipped the knot of the tie neatly up to his collar and reached for his jacket. 'Let's show the greedy bastard our posh interview room.'

'I think I'll go upstairs and wait for him there. I get better coffee up there anyway.'

He didn't have long to wait for the solicitor to appear and when he did it was obvious that he and Tollis had had words. John signed the documents after scanning them and he was almost certain that there had been no need for Smith to bring them himself. He'd used them as an excuse to come to the Kramer building to see Tollis about Maria Twarog.

Smith replaced them in his briefcase, refused coffee but apparently could not leave without voicing his opinions. 'I take exception to Mr Tollis's attitude—it may be an unwritten rule of etiquette, but it is unheard of to intrude between lawyer and client.'

John doubted if Tollis knew anything about etiquette. 'But your business with Maria was finished and she did choose to come to Sentinel.'

'I must say also I'm surprised you neglect your business to become involved with Sentinel affairs,' the lawyer said stiffly as he picked up his case. 'Mr Kramer left his business in your care . . .'

'That's really not your concern,' John pointed out, and Smith left in a state of huff.

Val had heard most of the exchange and looked amused.

'It would be comical if it wasn't so odd,' John said after Smith was gone. 'Unless he fancied the painting and swiped it for himself.'

'Hardly. He's a pillar of society.'

'Pillars have been known to sway and fall over,' John murmured. 'But I didn't mean it seriously—it's just odd that he should feel so strongly about Maria coming to us. Oh well, it will all blow over. What have you planned for me today?'

A lot of boring reading about what the various departments were currently involved in and it took him most of the morning to make a dent in it all. Investment, retail and standard management, research, etc., etc . . .

He skipped out for a late solitary lunch as a means of a break. Food was not really on his mind and he automatically turned into one of the closes near the office where there was a snack bar. He had to edge by a biker in black leather gear and crash helmet who was loitering on the gloomy steps, but he had no sooner gone by him when the man spun around and slammed John against the stone wall.

'Remember what I said on the phone, Leith?' The man was tall, with a heavy build that was emphasized by the leather jacket, and his face was hidden behind the dark visor of the helmet.

The suddenness of the attack had winded John. His head was ringing with the thud it had taken from the wall and he could feel the stinging of an open cut. Then anger surged and he shoved the man away. The leather gear and the helmet gave his attacker protection that he lacked, and when he swung a punch at the man's ribs it was absorbed by thick clothing and seemed to have no effect at all.

The man came back at him in a rush. 'Keep you bloody nose out of our affairs,' he growled. His fist caught John on the side of the head, the zip on the leather glove grazed his cheek but John automatically registered the fact that the man had said 'our'—there was more than one of them involved.

'This is just a warning,' his attacker went on as he sank a punch into the soft area under John's ribs. His weight pinned John against the wall and he could feel the sharp ridges of the stone wall pressing into his spine. Just yards away people were passing up the street, talking, not noticing the violence that was taking place in the shadows of the alley. John kicked out, tried to knee his attacker, and it was like fighting with a well-padded cushion. In return the man found his targets with ease and he had the weight behind the punches to make each one tell.

It was a losing battle from the start and there would have been more if Mike Cairns hadn't appeared. He took the downward steps in one leap and his huge hands reached for the jacket but he couldn't get a firm grip. The man dodged under his arms, ran for the exit of the close and an incoming couple came between him and Mike. There was a clumsy huddle of bodies, with Mike having to halt to save the young woman from falling over, apologies as he set her on her feet, and the next thing they heard was the roar of a motorbike. Mike cursed in disgust when he realized that the machine was gone before he had even got a look at it.

'You all right?'

John was trying to fill his lungs with air. He had been the meat in a sandwich, stuck between the man and the stone wall, and he knew that a lot of bruises would soon appear. He straightened up, felt the back of his head and his fingers came away with blood on them. 'I think so. It's a small cut.' His cheek was bleeding and his ear was numb.

'Come and have a pint,' he said.

Mike grinned. It was a rare sight and it changed him completely.

'And you can explain why you're following me around,' John added.

CHAPTER 4

He left Mike to order the drinks and sandwiches at the bar and went to the men's room to clean himself up. There was no serious damage, a graze on his cheek that might bruise, a swelling and small cut on his head that had already stopped bleeding, but the soft fleshy bits of his body were a different matter and would cause him pain later. And if Mike had not appeared it might have been much worse.

'I wasn't expecting it, not in daylight in a busy street,' he said as they ate beef sandwiches. 'He couldn't have known I would come out just then, so was he waiting in hope?'

Mike was nodding. 'He parked his machine around the corner but you can't hang about in that street. Probably he hoped you'd come and if you didn't he would have come back another time. But it also means he doesn't know of any other place when he can get at you. He's a very angry man, angry enough to take risks, and I don't like that.'

Mike drained his glass and set it down thoughtfully. 'He
took the trouble to hide his face but didn't rationalize what
he was doing—he could have been caught—I'd have had
him if that couple hadn't appeared. A man who isn't scared,
who attacks in daylight in a busy area . . . he's dangerous.'

'Bridie's boyfriend. He's worried that I'll find her. I
wonder if that means she's hiding from him too? She
sounded scared enough to take off.'

Mike didn't comment on that but went to fetch another
pint and when he came back John repeated the question
he'd asked earlier. 'How did you happen to be there? Has
Tollis asked you to follow me around?'

The big man shook his head. 'No.'

'I saw you outside Clare's flat last night.'

Mike shrugged. His features, which showed evidence of
other violent encounters, a broken nose and a couple of
small scars, gave nothing away and John had to let it go.
If Mike didn't want to explain there was nothing that would
force him. It was only a few months since his son Toby had
been killed while working on a case for Tollis and since
then Mike had closed in on himself. He came to work, did
whatever Tollis asked of him, but he was just as likely to
disappear for hours or days at a time. Tollis had remarked
that Mike was also drinking too much, but as long as he
was sober on the job there wasn't much he could do about
it.

John pushed the last sandwich towards him. 'I have to
get back. Val has loaded me up with reading matter and
I want to get through it so I can go down to Elmwood
tomorrow.'

'I'll be around,' was all Mike said.

'What did he mean?' John asked Tollis. He'd gone into
Sentinel to report what had happened and Tollis had
assessed the attacker in much the same way as Mike had.
Dangerous. Tollis had phoned and left a message for
Jamieson about the incident.

'God knows. I'm just letting him drift at the moment in

the hope that he'll snap out of it in time. I mentioned that
phone call you had; maybe he's transferred his attention to
you as a sort of son-replacement. In a way it's not a bad
thing, if you can put up with it. If you see him around just
ignore him.'

Jamieson came looking for him just after four. 'Well, Mr
Leith, what are you up to now?'
    There was surely no need for a man of his rank to check
on small beans like an interrupted assault, but John got the
feeling that Jamieson took a perverse pleasure in visiting
Kramer's. He sat in a comfortable chair after shedding his
overcoat and accepted the offer of a Scotch. He always gave
the impression of being only mildly interested in events,
with a laid-back attitude that was exaggerated by his soft
Highland accent. John sometimes wondered if he used the
accent to give exactly that impression.
    'Rees Kramer kept a stock of good stuff,' he said appreci-
atively, sipping malt from a chunky glass. 'I got Tollis's
brief message about what happened but I'd like to hear it
from you.'   `
    John went through it all. 'I suppose it was one of the men
involved in the burglaries—Bridie McGuire's boyfriend.'
    'Very likely. They're on to a good thing and don't want
anyone interested in their little informer, but they must
know we're getting close now that her involvement has been
twigged. It's the girl herself who concerns me, if they're
violent types, as it seems they possibly are. This business
today . . . it helps us to paint a picture of who we are
dealing with.' He sighed. 'They come to Edinburgh from
other parts of the country now and it makes life difficult.'
    'You think these men are outsiders?'
    'It's only a possibility. If so, they'll move the stuff out of
the city or store it until they feel like moving on. Nothing
has shown up yet from the very first incidents. They may
have worked this sort of thing elsewhere—we're checking,' he said, as he settled deeper into the chair. Jamieson
never gave the impression of working but John knew from

experience how sharp he was. 'The girl hasn't been in touch again?'

'No. I've spoken to her mother but she doesn't know anything.'

'If that young woman has led a sheltered life, more or less supporting her mother and with no social life . . .' Jamieson pondered and looked worried. 'She'd be easy to persuade, to forget her better instincts in the need for a bit of fun and excitement. But that wears off—if she has a conscience. She'll be very frightened now.' He stood up and reached for his coat. 'It's supposed to be the start of spring,' he grumbled as he pulled it on. At the door he paused. 'If she should phone again, tell her that we'll treat her with sympathy. Get her to come forward if you can.'

John was toying with the idea of leaving for Elmwood that night instead of the next day when the phone rang and he heard Mrs McGuire's frightened voice.

'A man was here looking for Bridie,' she said. 'He scared me. Why does he want Bridie? Has she done anything wrong?'

'What did he look like?'

'He stood in the shadows and I don't open the door properly after it's dark. He was dressed in dark clothes as well.'

'Did you see his face?'

'Not really, but I think he was a lot older than my daughter. He's not the sort of man I'd want her to go out with. What has she got herself into? I don't like people like that coming here.'

How to tell her enough to calm her down without causing her more worry? John did the best he could. 'I don't know. Maybe he's someone she met and didn't tell you about.'

'He didn't act like a friend of hers,' the woman said doubtfully.

'Well, you know how couples can fall out . . . He just asked where she was?'

'Demanded, as if he had the right to know. I don't know if he believed me when I said I had no idea where she went.' She sighed. 'I'm sorry to bother you, Mr Leith, but I thought you might have heard something.'

'You'll be the first to know,' John assured her, unwilling to offer false reassurances, because he was worried about the girl too.

He went on to join Tollis and gave him the details of the conversation and to chew over other thoughts that he had.

'Got another itch about this business?' Tollis asked.

'Sort of, but if it was the biker who paid Mrs McGuire a visit it has settled any doubts I had about this man.'

'In what way?'

'Well, when he phoned me, warning me off, I thought afterwards that I might be jumping to conclusions. He said I had been asking questions, poking about, and I assumed that he was talking about Bridie McGuire and it was only later that I realized he could have meant the other woman.'

'Now you know it's Bridie he's interested in.'

'Yes. Does it make sense, though?'

'Go on, I trust your hunches.'

John sighed and tried to put his reservations into words. 'From what Jamieson said, the men who are breaking into our properties are chancers. They would be delighted to have lists to work from, easy pickings in fact. Why get violent when Bridie ran away from them—if she did?'

'Maybe she took the lists with her.'

John felt deflated. 'That might do it,' he said.

'Is it likely that the man became threatening because you were also looking for Mrs Pearson? Why? Because of a painting and a few bits of jewellery?'

'No, you're right. I think I need a good night's sleep. I'm seeing mysteries where there are none.'

'One way to solve it: find both women,' Tollis said. 'But I'd concentrate on Bridie if I were you. Maria seemed in no great hurry to get her stuff back—she's probably gone off sightseeing.'

'Wonder how he knew I was looking for either of them? The trouble is that I've spoken to a lot of people: all of Mrs

Pearson's former neighbours, as well as Bridie's mother and the people she worked with. One of them must know that man.'

Tollis looked at his watch and John remembered he'd said he was going out. Then he noticed that the big man was not wearing his usual casual gear but a suit and a fresh shirt which showed gold cufflinks at the wrists. He also smelled of expensive aftershave.

'We'd need more men on the job if there are two separate inquiries and I've a sudden rush of business on my hands, so you'll have to cope as best you can. Three maritals came in in one day, would you believe?'

'I thought you didn't take them on any more?

'Sometimes—people still get divorced and it's business. Look, I've got to go—we'll talk about this in the morning.'

'Got a date?'

He was joking but Tollis nodded. 'Mm.' John wasn't sure if that meant yes, or if Tollis still had his mind on the two missing women. And as he made his way up to the flat on the top floor he tried to imagine the sort of woman who could get Tollis to leave his desk when it was piled high with paperwork.

The biker. The name stuck as the only means of identification and John still had him on his mind. Despite what Tollis said, he still wasn't totally convinced that the man would get violent because Bridie had skipped with the photocopies of the lists of empty properties. Why take the risk of attacking him in broad daylight, of going to speak directly to the girl's mother? Those questions bothered him well into the small hours and he decided that he would keep his options open and continue to look for both women, starting first thing in the morning. He didn't have to be at Elmwood until after lunch to take Gwen to the airport and Clare's idea of checking with the post office for a forwarding address for Mrs Pearson had been a good one. There were also all the other agencies like gas, electricity, Telecom, that people had to notify when they moved house—if they held on to the records and if they would give him the information. As for Bridie, there had to be other people who would know where she might run to.

The sun was streaming through the windows when he woke next morning, tempting him to pull on his running gear. He'd always run when he stayed at Elmwood, along the coast for miles when he was training for a race. Now it was purely for pleasure, to get the kinks out of limbs softened by office work, or just to sort out his thinking. He didn't jog. He took the downward slope of the Royal Mile at speed after the first limbering up, wincing as his bruises made themselves felt, then sweated his way through his usual route, pushing himself as if there was a winner's tape to be reached. The sun was just warm enough, even so early in the morning, to dry the dew from the grass. The pounding of his feet and his breathing were the only sounds but they didn't register. He was thinking about young Bridie McGuire. Where would such a girl go if she had no friends?

He turned and ran back the way he'd come and as soon as he reached the flat he rang Mrs McGuire's number. It was not yet eight but she answered right away. Maybe, like him, she was not sleeping well.

'I forgot to ask about relatives—is there anyone Bridie might go to visit, or old schoolfriends?'

'Some of my husband's people are still in Glasgow but we've lost touch. And I don't know about schoolfriends— she never mentioned any recently. I'll have a think about it and let you know.'

He apologized for bothering her but she sounded much calmer than the night before. He showered and changed. For once, Val was late for work so he set about phoning the post office and others who might have Mrs Pearson's address. They didn't give out that kind of information, they told him. Try writing, but even then . . .

Tollis had not arrived either so there was no help from him. In the end he drove back to the street where he still had the small shop to visit.

'Mrs Pearson? I knew her by sight but she only bought

the odd pint of milk here. The old lady she worked for preferred supermarkets—it was her one excitement of the week to drive out to one of them on a Saturday. Why not see the district nurse who went in most days—or the minister? She was a great churchgoer.'

He had no idea where to find the district nurse but the minister knew Mrs Pearson well. 'She was very helpful at our jumble sales. A great knitter. I think she was going to live with her sister, or was it her sister-in-law? Sorry I can't be sure.'

Her name? He shook his head, doubted if he'd ever heard it.

And there were an awful lot of Pearsons in the phone book . . .

John drove to Elmwood feeling frustrated and found boxes in the hall which Janet told him sadly were the things suitable for charity shops.

'I didn't realize how much there would be. The other things are in his study and I thought you'd be the one to go through his desk.' She looked tired and on edge.

John put his arm around her shoulders. 'There wasn't any need to do this now. I'll finish it.'

They were disposing of Rees's life, all the things that were the man, but there was no need to strip the house bare. His books and pictures would still fill the rooms, just as his invisible footprints were on every carpet.

'Leave the study and anything else for me to do— why don't you invite your sister down here to keep you company?'

Janet considered that. 'Maybe you're right,' she said. 'I didn't think it would bother me, but I'm dreading Gwen leaving. I was used to being on my own a lot, but now . . .' She drew herself up and then spoke briskly. 'I'll phone Sheila and see if she'll come. She's a great one for the shops and we'll have a bit of a holiday.'

He went into Rees's study and made a start on it while lunch was being prepared, but first he threw open the windows before turning to the desk. Reluctantly he opened

each drawer in turn and found them all tidy with containers
for paperclips, pens, stationery. It was a jolt to see his
uncle's beautiful copperplate handwriting in the leather-
bound diary, each appointment set out in neat detail. Most
of what he found he replaced for his own use, but in the
last drawer was an old biscuit tin with a dented lid. He ran
his finger over the sticky label with its faded writing and
remembered the day he'd presented it to Rees.

He had been eleven and had just won his first race and
he'd been surprised to find his uncle at the finishing line.
The next day Rees had presented him with a stop watch,
'so you can time your practice runs.' The gift had been
given matter-of-factly, almost as an afterthought, but it had
seen him through university, through so many training runs
after that.

And at the time he'd felt obliged to give this strange new
guardian something in return and the only possession he
valued was a model yacht he'd made, a replica, in fact, of
the one his parents had died in. He'd wrapped it up carefully and put it in the old tin box and here it still was after
all these years. Had Rees valued the gift, or had he put it
out of sight in the bottom drawer? He hoped he knew the
answer. Rees never kept anything unless it was of value to
him. He took out the model and found something else;
packed in tissue was the small trophy he'd won that first
day.

'Lunch,' Janet said, poking her head around the door
and John replaced the tin in the drawer, feeling sad that
Rees had never put his feelings into words. It must have
been a painful affliction, to feel affection, pride, or even
love, but never be able to show it.

'It's not an easy job,' Janet said, glancing at him as she
moved back and forth in the kitchen. 'He'll always be here,
no matter how much stuff we clear out—but I don't suppose that will bother you.'

'No,' John said. Not now it wouldn't.

He and Gwen left right after lunch for the drive to Turnhouse. She looked relieved to be going.

'You didn't explain what happened to your face, little brother, and if Janet hadn't been so busy thinking about Rees she would have asked.'

'I bumped into something,' he said.

Gwen made a sound of disbelief. 'Someone's fist, I expect. It's time you took a course in self-defence.' Then she frowned. 'I wish you'd stay away from Tollis. It was bad enough when Uncle Rees was part of it all, but you don't have the same . . . attitude.'

'You can remember when Rees worked with Tollis? I was never all that interested in the firm and then they split the business up—and what do you mean, attitude?'

'They were probably trained for one thing, in the army. You're an accountant, not a sleuth, private eye, or whatever it is that Tollis enjoys doing. You used to be satisfied with your pages of figures; now I don't know what you get up to. Isn't running the business a big enough challenge for you?'

She turned worried eyes towards him. 'I just don't like to see you with cuts and bruises. I want to see you married, living at Elmwood, being an ordinary man, husband, father . . . Settled down, for God's sake!'

There was no answer to that, and after a few moments he heard Gwen sigh, then laugh under her breath. 'Sorry. Big sister beating the drum again. But you know what I mean.'

He did indeed. It was an eminently sensible plan for his life but not one that he could see happening in the near future, especially the bit about being married. Clare had her own views on that. The rest he might manage, one of these days.

He saw Gwen off on her flight home to Aberdeen, then drove leisurely back to the city. He hadn't noticed the grey Volvo that had followed him all the way from Elmwood and he didn't see it now. He was too busy thinking about the model yacht in the biscuit tin in his uncle's desk.

CHAPTER 5

He left the car at the side of Kramer House because he intended going to Clare's later, and found a note on his desk saying that Val had phoned to apologize for being absent, a small domestic crisis. The work of the day seemed to have functioned without either of them.

He filled the afternoon with clearing his desk and by the time he was finished he realized that everyone had gone home. There were still lights on in the building and he could hear the sound of cleaners working in various rooms. They tended to shout to each other, leaning over the banister rails with comments like, 'Tea-break in ten minutes?'

'The kettle's already on—oh, sorry sir, didn't know you were still here.'

It was a different life after six o'clock when a different regime operated. The corridors were full of vacuum cleaners and plastic sacks of rubbish; music from radios played loudly and he found himself slipping down the stairs to Sentinel like an intruder. The women who cleaned never met those who made the mess and when the day staff turned up they took the smell of polish for granted, he thought.

'I don't let them in here,' Tollis said with a yawn. He had his chair tilted dangerously against the wall. 'I wait till it looks like a tip and then decant for a while now and then.'

John looked around and wondered when the next decanting was due. 'I hope you pay them overtime.'

'I didn't expect you back—thought you might stay with Janet over the weekend.'

'I'm taking David out tomorrow. Anything new happening?'

'We're looking for bugs in that new office block along the road. They think their board meetings are being leaked— it's probably a director on the take.' He yawned again,

rubbed his eyes and let his chair fall forward with a bang.
'I need some coffee.'

'Were you up all night again?' John asked as he poured
from the jug that was permanently on the hotplate. The
liquid was so strong that it came out thick.

'Told you, looking for bugs. It's easier when the place is
empty and only a few people know what we're about—the
bloody things shouldn't be sold on the open market.'

'Thought you had a date?'

'Something came up,' he said evasively.

'That's what Val said as well. There was a note to say she
had a domestic crisis and couldn't come in this morning.' It
wasn't meant to be a speculation on his part. He hadn't
consciously connected the two events at all, but now he
saw Tollis was embarrassed and wished he hadn't said
anything. Val and Tollis? Well, they had both worked in
the building for years so they must know each other very
well.

'Sorry,' he said. 'I wasn't fishing.'

'Nothing to fish for,' Tollis grunted and that was all he
would say on the subject.

'I just came down to tell you I'd be at Clare's and not
around much for the rest of the weekend.'

They arranged that they would leave notes if anything
cropped up and when John got to his car he found a note
of another kind under the windscreen wiper.

*This is the last warning, Leith. Either leave things be or you'll
be sorry*, it said. It had been written in a hurry on a page
torn from a diary but it meant that someone had been
around when he got out of the car; had probably been
following him. That would mean the man knew where Elmwood was as well. He screwed the piece of paper up and
stuffed it in his pocket and made sure that no one followed
him to Clare's flat. He had to take the cryptic message
seriously but it smacked of coming from a man who was
getting slightly obsessed.

Clare noticed the cut on his cheek right away and
touched it with her fingers. 'Trouble?'

Since the shooting incident she became quiet when there was any mention of violence, even on the television news, although she tried not to show it. So he played down his bruise.

'Nothing, just bumped it,' he said and she nodded absently, accepting the lie easily.

She was not a moody person, but there were times when she was preoccupied and that evening was one of them. Sometimes it was simply because she'd had a heavy day, but this evening he knew that it was something more than that and had begun before he arrived. She hadn't changed out of her office clothes and she was in a pensive mood at the supper table. So he tried to lift her mood by telling her about Val and her possible relationship with Tollis.

'I saw them together once,' she said. 'They made a nice couple, sort of settled, as if they'd been married a long time and were comfortable with each other.'

'You never mentioned it.'

She was thoughtful. 'Tollis is such a private man—I felt I shouldn't have seen them. I just put it out of my mind.' It was exactly how he'd expect her to feel. And knowing her so well, he knew he couldn't ask what was bugging her —that she'd reveal it in her own good time.

They watched television, an episode of a serial that she enjoyed but he knew that her attention wasn't on it. In the end she switched it off and came back to curl up beside him.

'You know I've been getting promotion reports for the last two years? Well, it's finally come through and I'm going up a grade.'

'That's great.'

'Yes. But it means that I'll probably be transferred. I've been thinking about it ever since I was told and I've decided that I want the promotion.'

'Ah.' He tried to imagine what it would be like knowing that she was no longer just half an hour away at any time of the day, and couldn't.

'You have to accept the transfer, then?'

'If I turn it down I stay at the same rank.' She was quite calm about her decision and he knew that it had troubled her to make it. She pressed her body closer and spoke with her head against his chest.

'I wasn't sure how to tell you but I've worked it out. If it's London I'll commute. Lots of people do, for the weekends.'

London was remote, in another country for Christ's sake, foreign, hours away in train or plane, but Clare was free to choose. Damn the bloody unspoken rules of their relationship. He loved her and didn't want her off in London of all places.

'It could be somewhere much closer, of course, but it's best to think of the worst,' she said, moving her head to look up to see if he agreed.

'The very worst,' he said, nodding his head like a puppet.

They made love as if it was Clare's last night before departing for people and places unknown, when in fact it might be weeks before that happened. It removed the tension and in the morning they were both tired with a surfeit of physical pleasure.

'Nice,' she said, as they lingered in the warm bed with the duvet wrapped around both so that they looked like one long sausage. 'But I'll have to get up or I'll be late for the hairdresser.'

'Mm,' he agreed. 'We could save time if we share the shower.'

But no time was saved. Mutual soaping and drying only revived the desire of the night and he was astounded, as always, that the feeling never got any less intense. And he might be about to lose all of it, if her job took her away from him. He thought of what Gwen had said, about settling down at Elmwood, and knew that it wasn't the time to mention it to Clare.

Saturday usually meant they could take things easy, but he'd an appointment at David's school and shopping to do for the camping holiday. Then he was taking his son out for lunch, probably at a hamburger place for double helpings of everything followed by milk shakes. A trip to the cinema might follow.

'And I'm going out with the girls tonight, late back, I expect,' Clare said. There was no hint of tiredness in her eyes, just a lingering softness that was also in her lips as he kissed her.

David seemed to grow by inches every time he saw him now. The long legs already showed a gap between trousers and shoes, the sleeves of his blazer were the same. He was excited about the camp and wanting the same gear as his friends, so the first stop was a sports shop. The packages were loaded into the car and then they ate.

'I brought my camera—can we go to the Zoo?'

Anywhere that meant they would be in a crowd, John thought, and since it was a lovely, crisp, sunny day, the Zoo was as good as anywhere. Still, he was uneasy when he stood behind David who was taking snaps of the big cats. If the biker took off the disguising leathers he could be any one of the crowd, standing at John's elbow, following in his footsteps. The only features he would recognize were the man's height and his build. He kept a lookout for a man on his own and as they waited for the keeper to arrive with the animals' meat, he heard a quiet voice speak in his ear.

'Better get the boy back to school. You were followed.'

Mike Cairns was a pace away, just one of the crowd, and he was looking not at John but past him at the arrival of the keeper. No one would guess they knew each other. It was neatly done, and John edged David out of the crush of people, his heart rate speeding up but copying Mike's example and not showing any interest in those around him.

'I've got to get to an appointment,' he told his son as they walked down to the main gates and the short distance to where the car was parked. 'We'll come again another time.'

The prospect of leaving for the camp in two days' time over-rode any disappointment his son might have felt and on the drive back to school he chattered about camp fires and sleeping in a tent. John tried to keep an eye on following traffic but he didn't know what he was looking for and it was a relief when he saw David into the confines of the school grounds. Just before he left, David asked if they could visit his grandfather the next day.

'I told him about the camp when he phoned and he was sorry we wouldn't see him at Easter. And I won't get to see Sheba for ages if we don't go tomorrow.'

Albert Gumley, John's father-in-law, had given David the dog in the first place and took care of her now that the boy was a boarder but he used it as an enticement to see his grandson outside the stipulated visiting times. John had to grit his teeth and comply because David was still young enough to take adults at face value, seeing nothing of the underlying dislike that they might have for each other. An irritable peace was kept by these visits but it was a peace that Gumley did nothing to promote. He had taken the news of Rees's death with barely concealed pleasure, needling John with the gibe that he was still around, surviving, when Rees Kramer was not.

'Can we go?' David pleaded.

'If you get permission. They may want you to get your packing done.'

He drove back to the office, hoping that Tollis would be around and that more than likely Mike would head there too. He wanted to know who Mike had spotted and if he'd been able to get a good look at him this time.

He was angry that he'd been followed when he had David along. Someone had been in his shadow as he'd gone through town, maybe he'd been in the same fast food place. All the time he and David had been eating, there had been this other person looking on; a voyeur who . . . had what in mind? He didn't like the thought that violence could have erupted with David there to witness it, maybe even be involved in it. And he was grateful for the school camp that would take his son to the remoteness of northern Scotland for the next week. The man had already displayed

an obsessional anger that made no sense and that sort of
irrational behaviour didn't consider the innocent.

'He was still in his biker's gear, well back, but keeping
you in sight,' Mike reported. 'I don't know where he parked
his machine—I was just making sure he didn't get close to
you so I stayed at your back. We'll have to give you some
lessons in spotting a tail.'

'And self-defence,' Tollis put in, but John shook his head.
'I'm no hero, I'd run.' That raised a laugh but it quickly
died.

'He was content to watch,' Mike added. 'There were a
few other bikers there, in groups with girls, so he didn't
stand out in that leather gear. He was carrying his helmet
but his collar was up and I only got a sight of him from a
distance. Longish dark hair, sallow skin, mid-thirties I'd
guess. I only picked him out because he was so obviously
intent on every move you made. Wonder what he was up
to?'

'Let's play around with ideas.' Tollis walked up and
down as he always did when he wanted to think clearly and
now he held up one finger. 'First, he has an interest in what
John's been doing and warns him about keeping his nose
out of his business—and I suppose we'd better widen that
to mean that by looking for either Bridie McGuire or Mrs
Pearson the housekeeper, John is stepping on his toes.' He
held up a second finger. 'Two, he's checking to see if you've
been scared off and since you are doing something innocuous like taking your boy out for the day, he's prepared to
watch and leaves you alone. From that he may also be
reassured for a while, but I wouldn't bank on it.'

A third finger. 'At the bottom of all this he is scared that
you'll discover something and so prevent him from doing
. . . what?'

'Money,' Mike said. 'The biggest motive of all. He's got
an investment and John's threatening to cut off his supply.'

Tollis sat heavily in his chair again. 'We knew that in
the first place if it's Bridie he's concerned about. I can't
fathom where Mrs Pearson might have a connection to him.

We should look for both women just in case—or nail him. And John, you'll have to be careful because he's got a fixation that you're the danger: only you.'

'I'm not changing my plans to accommodate him—I may be taking David to see Gumley tomorrow.' He got quick glances of alarm which were understandable. Albert Gumley had once been an active godfather-type figure in Edinburgh, known to the police but never convicted. Having him as a father-in-law had made life difficult, mainly because the old man had wanted custody of his grandson and had never forgiven John for defying him. 'It will be a short visit, in daylight.'

Neither Tollis nor John looked at Mike but they expected a response and it wasn't long in coming. 'Don't ask me to go with you. I can't stand the man,' he growled. 'He should have died months ago; what's keeping him alive?'

'Sheer malice, but at least it's all in his mind. His criminal activities are over and if you believe in retribution, Gumley is having more than his share of suffering now. David doesn't understand and it's weird to see them together—Gumley cares for him, in his fashion. We'll be safe enough inside those walls.'

'And our friend seems to prefer a motorbike to get around on—but that doesn't mean he doesn't use a car. I think the biker's gear is just a good disguise; it suits him for the moment.'

'Whatever is going on it hasn't put an end to the break-ins. Jamieson has had two more reported and I've had to take men off other things to organize a patrol of sorts. They'll move around the properties in rotation but it's still a hit-and-miss solution.'

'When did you hear?'

'He phoned at lunch-time. He thinks they're making their final killing, but in his opinion it will make them easier to catch. They're getting cocky and he thinks they'll do one too many—the longer they spend in a house, the more likely a neighbour will get suspicious. If they do any more of our properties it will cost us business when word gets out. A security firm is supposed to provide security and at the moment we're failing badly. And,' he went on gloomily, 'our premiums will go up.'

He and Mike began to discuss their work schedules in more detail and John left them to it. He phoned Gumley's house to let them know he'd be there the next day with David and then took a call from Janet.

'There was a phone call for you this afternoon from Rees's lawyer, Mr Smith. When I said you were staying in town he sounded a bit put out but he said he'd ring you at the office on Monday.'

John groaned inwardly. Smith was turning into an old woman and he'd have to do something about the future handling of the Kramer affairs. He put it out of his mind and asked Janet if her sister had agreed to come to keep her company.

'Yes, it's all arranged. She's coming on Monday.'

He picked David up after lunch the next day to drive to Cramond where Gumley lived, with a detour to one of the supermarkets that opened on Sundays to buy a treat for the dog and 'something for Grandfather'. The boy was excited about seeing his dog and John gloomily reflected that he would then be alone with Gumley and his nurse-cum-houseperson, Garek.

The gates stood open because they were expected. Gumley had security in the grounds, cameras in the trees, no doubt, to guard his fiercely desired privacy. Did the neighbours know who lived so close to them, John wondered, as the car kicked up the weedless gravel of the drive? Did they send Christmas cards to the poor old man who was housebound, never guessing that Gumley had no good wishes for anyone?

Garek stood in the doorway before they left the car, his thin figure dressed in white shirt, black trousers and waistcoat. Under his bald head, his features, usually sombre, were now cracked into a smile as David raced up the steps clutching his supermarket bag.

'Where's Sheba?'

'In the kitchen. Say hello to your grandfather first.' As usual Garek spoke without any accent. He had taken trouble over his English lessons at some point in the past and now rarely used idioms or the shortened words that slip so easily off the tongue of a native. Hence there were no clues to where he originated.

David knew the way and didn't seem bothered by the heat of the house, but John knew what to expect and slipped out of his sports jacket and carried it over one arm. Gumley liked to keep the central heating on high and there was always a fire in the sitting-room, even in midsummer. The old man was sitting beside it, a blanket draped over his shoulders and another across his knees. His face grew more gaunt every day; his cheeks were sunken and shrivelled, the skin as grey as a corpse's, but the life force was there in the eyes which fastened on David as soon as he entered the room.

The contrast between the very young and the very old was vivid, with the boy running easily across the room towards his grandfather. He dropped the chocolates in his lap and then put his arm gently around the old man's shoulders. It was instinctively done, as if he knew that the body under his arm was fragile, and to anyone looking on it made a touching picture, but John had mixed feelings. In the end it was pride in his son's naïve compassion that won over distaste.

Gumley fingered the chocolate box. It was impossible to tell from his expression how he felt about the gift except that he clutched it with skeletal fingers, nodding a thank-you.

'Can I see Sheba now—take her out?'

The boy's cheeks were like rosy apples, his eyes were bright, his dark hair shone and Gumley's eyes lingered on his face as if envying the body that was bursting with freshness and good health.

'Garek will show you where she is,' he said in a voice husky with the overflow of liquid from his inefficient lungs.

That left John alone with him, a situation he suffered

every time he visited the house, but one he never got used to. It required good acting to seem at ease so that the old man got no satisfaction from his discomfort.

'It's only a short visit. David has to get ready to leave tomorrow.'

Gumley nodded, drooping now that he no longer had the stimulus of his grandson in the room, but it was only a physical reaction, the eyes still sparked.

'You've got your hands on the lot, then, Rees Kramer's wealth and his business. How are you going to cope with it all, I wonder? How long before you realize that you're not like your uncle?'

As usual, he had found a weakness to probe. John didn't answer but that didn't seem to bother Gumley. Probably he didn't expect an answer.

'You see—' Gumley paused to suck in air—'Rees liked it, the game of making money, just as I did, although we chose different methods. Rees and I . . . we had the same mentality and if he hadn't managed it honestly, who knows, he might have tried it my way.' Gumley laughed, a rattle that was nauseating. 'And he knew it—that's why he disliked me so much. I was a mirror image.'

He looked up at John from under hooded eyes, hoping perhaps for an angry denial, but in fact John felt that there was some truth in what he said. Rees had enjoyed power and wealth but the difference was that he hadn't boasted about it, or clutched for it in the way that Gumley had.

'And don't think your uncle stuck to the letter of the law —he saw nothing wrong with a little legal manipulation if it suited him—and now it's all wasted on you.' Gumley turned away as if the sight of his son-in-law in his living-room was something he could do without.

A log shifted in the fire and fell in a shower of sparks and Gumley looked at it with irritation. 'Put on some more,' he ordered as if afraid of a drop in temperature. John obeyed, lifting the tinder-dry logs with fire-irons and he could feel Gumley watching him. And as he straightened up he saw David and the dog out in the grounds, with Garek walking a few yards behind them. The sound of the boy's laughter reached into the room and he saw Gumley turn his head to the sound—there was no doubt that the man did indeed have some feeling for the boy, incredible as it seemed that Gumley could feel emotional about any living thing.

'You'll never do it,' Gumley continued as if there had been no interruption, 'manage it like Rees did.'

'Probably not,' John agreed. 'But I'll take advice.'

His lack of argument took the wind out of Gumley's sails. 'You need Garek, then—he's clever. Did you know that he was once on the side of the law?'

He watched John's reaction with the ghost of a smile. 'Yes, Garek was a solicitor once and I'd trust no other of that brigade. He's worked well for me.' Gumley's eyes had lost interest and his head drooped.

John left the room and went outside to watch the dog and boy romp in the chilly sunshine and after a bit Garek joined him. John explained that Gumley was sleeping and Garek nodded as if he wasn't surprised.

'It's good for him,' the man said, with his eyes still following David. 'I think that one day he will not wake up, soon maybe.' It was said calmly enough and John wondered what Garek would do then, with no master to watch over. And as if the man guessed he explained that the house had already been signed over to him.

'Your son will inherit the rest,' he said without looking at John, knowing already how John felt about the sort of money it was.

'I didn't know you had once been a lawyer,' John said, changing the subject.

'A long time ago.' Garek turned his cold grey eyes on him. 'Maybe I will be again . . .' His mouth twitched. 'I have had a wide experience.'

Then his eyes went past John, focused on the distant gates at the end of the drive. 'There is a motorbike, a Harley Davidson, that has twice gone past and each time it has slowed as it passed the gate.'

John could still hear the low growl of its engine and he

walked quickly across the grass towards David and told
him it was time to leave. Garek was curious.

'Someone you know?'

'How did you know the type of bike he was riding?'
John asked as David took the dog through the house to the
kitchen.

'I have an interest in motorbikes. I have a collection—
I'll show you one day if you are really interested—but why
are you so concerned about that one?'

John hesitated and then gave a brief explanation as
David ran ahead. In the past Garek had been helpful,
smoothing over difficult patches by handling Gumley tact-
fully, and although there was no doubt where his loyalty
lay, Garek had an underlying reasonableness to his nature.
It showed now, for as soon as he described how the man
on the motorbike had been following him, Garek's manner
changed, mainly because David might be in some sort of
danger.

'I'll get out the car and follow you back to town,' he said,
moving with a purpose, and John heard him issuing orders
to another unseen male member of the household to watch
over Mr Gumley. Garek kept his word and drove behind
him all the way back to David's school and parked outside
the gates while John saw his son safely into the hands of
his housemaster.

'He veered off when he realized we were together,' Garek
commented when John rejoined him. 'That is quite an
expensive model he rides, in the lower price range maybe,
but they are all costly machines. In fact, I have one like it
myself.'

'Is it the sort of machine that is easily recognizable?
Would he need to use a specialist supplier for parts, or a
certain garage?'

Garek knew what he was getting at. 'There should be no
problem in tracing it, or the man,' Garek said thoughtfully.
'I don't know how popular that sportster model is, but even
so, there cannot be very many. But I will make inquiries
—life can be boring and I would enjoy doing this.' He

looked past John at the school buildings. 'I will be here tomorrow when the children leave, just to make sure that our friend is not around, but if you are the target I don't think we need worry about the boy.' He rarely said as much as he did that day and John wondered where Garek originated from and decided that Eastern Europe was the most likely.

'Thanks,' he said, and Garek nodded to show that he understood he meant it.

'I'm surprised that you like motorbikes,' John said. 'I didn't think you had much free time.'

'For the Harleys? I'll tell you about them sometime, Mr Leith. One day I will . . . what is it they say? I will put on the shades and head for the sun.' He was smiling as he drove away, leaving John open-mouthed with astonishment. Garek had driven in the opposite direction, back to Cramond and there was no sign of a motorbike. A strange man, he thought, to care for Gumley all these years and yet he'd retained something that Gumley had lost—if Gumley had ever had a touch of decency in his make-up.

He headed for Clare's flat but drove carefully, checking to make sure that he wasn't being followed. What sort of man was the biker? What could be so threatening that he felt obliged to know what John was doing? And what did he intend to do if he caught up with him in some private place? Garek might prove to be a big help if he could trace the bike or provide some clue to the man's identity.

The lights were with him as he crossed Princes Street and headed up the Mound and the biker was suddenly there too. He came out of nowhere, up on John's right, stayed with him although he could easily have surged ahead, and half way up the hill he brought the bike close in. He turned his head, face as usual hidden behind the visor, and slowly he raised his right hand, cocked a finger as if it was an imaginary gun. He pointed it, held his position for moments more, then roared off ahead. He indicated a right turn and as John crossed the junction he could see the bike far up the street on the right that led to the Castle.

The man had made his point. The finger could have been a real gun, his target an easy one.

Then he had disdainfully ridden off as if to say 'Fuck you, John Leith, I don't need to find out where you're going because I already know where you work, where you live and where you play.' It was a further display of the man's character, a two-fingered gesture that showed he was going to be persistent, was serious about his threat, and it was a promise of more to come. He was also brimful of confidence.

John drove on to Clare's flat and later, while she had a bath, he checked that all the doors and windows had good security locks.

CHAPTER 6

He was late getting to work the next morning and the bad start to the day was how it seemed set to continue. For one thing, the good spell of weather was over and the city was dampened by a cold layer of fog; the sort of dampness that penetrated the warmest of clothes. They had to keep the lights on in the office and it affected everyone's enthusiasm for work, if such a thing existed on a Monday morning.

Val was short-tempered and he heard her snap at the girls in the outer office and the last straw was when Smith phoned, asking once more for Maria's address in Edinburgh. In exasperation, John gave it but explained, 'She's not here, she's touring around, and as far as I know she checked out of that guest house.'

'Well, I have good news for her. If she contacts you will you tell her that I have her belongings and she can collect them from my office.' One up for Ambrose and didn't his smugness echo across the phone lines.

'You found Mrs Pearson, then?' John said.

'She was never missing. My secretary simply hadn't filed her new address. I dislike loose ends and I'm glad that my client can now claim the rest of her inheritance. Mr Tollis can close that file.'

So that was that, John thought as he hung up the phone. Tollis had been right and the biker hadn't been protecting Mrs Pearson after all because the housekeeper, according to Smith, had never been lost. He had to be Bridie's boyfriend, either protecting his investment or looking for her if she had taken off in fright. So why the hell was he issuing threats? None of it rang true, despite all the arguments that were presenting themselves to tell him otherwise.

'In a pig's eye.' The biker was not acting. He was frantically trying to divert John's attention elsewhere and something more than housebreaking had to be at stake. And to find what it was he had to find Bridie McGuire. Where the hell was she?

He couldn't think of any way he could trace her and he couldn't concentrate on work. He stood by the window, wondering what he was doing, getting involved with detective work and thinking with regret of more carefree days when he was his own boss. His accountancy business had been neglected when Rees took ill and eventually he had transferred all his clients over to Kramer accountants. Also, his flat in Stockbridge had been put up for sale but the market was slow and there had been no firm offers for it. For the sake of something positive to do, he phoned the lawyer who was handling the sale, a young man called Ian Lambert. After all, he still had a business to run.

'I've been meaning to call you,' Ian Lambert said. 'I think we've got a nibble and you may even get your price. Not bad considering the way the market has been going.'

'How are you on company set-ups?' John asked on impulse.

'What do you have in mind?'

'Advice about some changes here at Kramer's.'

'Wow. How about having lunch together one day, then?'

'Er, today might be better if you're free. I want to check on some ideas before I attend a meeting tomorrow.'

They made a date for one o'clock and John smiled at

Lambert's enthusiasm as he hung up the phone. They must be about the same age and therefore rather young to be taken seriously by the big boys of the city.

He already knew the basics of how he wanted to restructure the company and he'd intended to look for a more senior man to handle it, but if Ian proved capable . . . why not? And Smith wouldn't like losing the company's business. That made the day seem a little brighter.

He went down to talk over the events of the previous day with Tollis before going out to meet Ian. 'And Garek says he'll keep in touch about the motorbike.'

Tollis was amused. 'Imagine him having a collection of motorbikes. I always fancied a Goldwing myself,' he said, with a faraway look in his eyes. 'See if you can wangle me an invitation to see them.'

'What about Smith? He's crowing because he found Mrs Pearson and we couldn't.'

Tollis grimaced. 'He'll charge that girl a fat fee, too. At least he's off my back.'

John looked at his watch. Still an hour to go before he had to meet the young lawyer but he felt too restless to hang about the office and Tollis sensed it.

'What's bothering you?'

'I don't know. Yes I do, I'm angry. I feel that someone's pulling the wool over my eyes and the biker is hanging around laughing. He keeps popping up but so far the threats have been empty. And that damned girl doesn't realize what she's done.'

'It's called frustration,' Tollis said calmly. 'It's upon all of us when the trail peters out, until the next thing develops. You have to work on something else and learn patience.'

'To hell with it. I'm going to look for a birthday present for Clare,' John said, striding out of the office, out of the building.

'Watch your back,' Tollis called after him, but it was said with a chuckle.

He didn't need the warning. Once more he was in the situation of suspecting everyone in the crowds on the street, of not knowing if this face or that one belonged to the man who liked to hide behind a biker's helmet or if the biker meant half of what he said.

There was a jeweller in Rose Street he'd used before and that was where he headed. The small window was full of glittering items, but Clare was not the glittering type. She liked gold and in the end he chose a bracelet of linked petal shapes.

'Any engraving?' the girl asked. She put the bracelet on her own wrist to show him how it looked and he liked the way the raised design caught and reflected light. He shook his head. Any message that went with the bracelet would be said aloud. He slipped the flat box into his pocket and set off for the nearby pub where he was lunching with Ian. The fog lay close to the ground and the castle, high up on its rock, loomed eerily out of it. There was no sign of the biker.

Ian Lambert looked more like a large schoolboy than a lawyer, with sandy hair and freckles and the body of a rugby player. He disposed of the food quickly and then got down to business.

'Have you any ideas of your own?'

'Well, Rees owned the shares and ran the business himself—I want a more flexible management. In fact, I want to be very much in the background but retaining control, if you see what I mean.'

'Simple enough. Just set up a board of directors, from your own staff if you like, choose an overall manager, and give yourself the title of chairman.'

John grinned. It was exactly what he'd had in mind and he discussed the fine details for another half-hour, drank a few beers, and then asked if Ian would consider taking over Kramer's affairs.

'I'm a bit junior for that but I'll have a word with the senior partners—they'll kiss your hand, I expect.' He hesitated. 'What's wrong with the firm you've got?'

'I don't like the man much. In business-speak I suppose

you'd call it a clash of personalities. Ambrose Smith is the one I mean.'

Ian seemed surprised. 'He's quality. It's my ambition to reach the same dizzy heights, or at least to make his sort of income.' He leaned back in the wooden chair, put his arms behind his head and a dreamy look came into his eyes. 'A villa in Florida, another in Portugal somewhere . . . yes, I'd like his lifestyle.'

'But he works alone—how come he can do enough to earn it?'

Ian assumed a knowing look. 'That's what I've heard others ask but he only takes on class clients—like your company. He's not a court lawyer, more a trust fund and family type, but only takes on the best. The thing is to develop a reputation and he's certainly done that.'

'Pity about his personality,' John murmured, thinking of Smith's efforts to grab Maria back on his books.

Satisfied with the plans they'd discussed, he felt more prepared for the meeting that was planned for the next morning. Back at the office he was just in time to take a phone call from Maria Twarog. She sounded happy, bubbling with the news that she was enjoying her holiday.

'Can I come to see you?'

'Your lawyer phoned just this morning to say that he had found the housekeeper—he's holding the painting and the rest of the things at his office, ready for you to collect.'

'Oh.' It didn't seem important to her any more. 'Can I see you anyway? I want to ask a favour. I'm here to pick up some things, then I'm going off to see more of the scenery up north and I don't want to keep paying rent on a room here unless I have to, so I wondered if I could leave some of my things at the Agency. I think a backpack would give me more freedom and if I could leave my suitcases somewhere safe . . . I bought a lot of new clothes . . .' She ran out of breath and laughed and he thought it was amazing what a holiday and a shopping spree had done for her morale.

'How about I pick you up and bring your stuff back here?' he suggested. It wasn't part of Sentinel's brief to act as a left-luggage department but there was no harm in doing her a favour. The address was the one she'd given them already, a small guest house in Newington, and he arranged to be there in half an hour.

'I'm going out for a bit,' he told Val. 'If Bridie McGuire should phone, try to get an address from her.'

Val looked startled and then puzzled and John remembered that she'd been out of the office when he found Bridie's name on the list. 'She's the one we think has been leaking the information about the properties,' he told her.

'I didn't realize you'd managed to pin it down,' she said. She looked very pale and John wondered if the small crisis that had kept her off work had in fact been an illness. She'd been very quiet in the past few days, too.

'Are you all right, Val?'

'Yes.' She sounded prickly, and he sighed. She was the sort of woman who would never admit to any weakness and while he guessed it was a defence mechanism of long standing—Rees's fault—it was an attitude that could put other people's backs up. If she came over like that at the next day's meeting . . .

'I shouldn't be long,' he said. But he was delayed in getting away because someone had parked badly across the entrance to the parking area and he had to go back to the Sentinel office to find the culprit.

Maria's address was only a few minutes' drive away but as he neared the guest house, he saw a crowd of people grouped on the pavement.

'There was an accident,' someone said. 'That poor girl . . .'

'It was no accident,' said another. 'The bloody fool ran right up on the pavement and mowed her down.'

John pushed his way to the front and saw the scattered luggage first, then Maria lying on her side. Her clothes were torn and dirty and there was a bad graze on her face. A couple of women were bending over her and because she was so pale, he thought at first that she was dead. One of the woman saw his expression and assured him that she was still breathing.

'Someone has phoned for an ambulance,' one woman said. 'She's got blood coming from her ear—I don't think we should move her. That man saw what happened and he said if the car hadn't hit her cases first it might have been worse.' She was trying to offer some sort of comfort but John could only stare down at the unconscious girl. He pulled off his jacket and draped it over Maria and at the same time heard the scream of the approaching ambulance. He could feel his own blood pounding in his ears and his face felt stiff. It was a coincidence, but it was so like the way his wife had been killed that it was only much later that he realized he hadn't asked what sort of vehicle had hit Maria.

'I know her,' he told the ambulance men. 'Which hospital are you taking her to?'

They told him it would be the Royal at first. 'To the accident unit.'

'I'll follow you, then,' he said.

It had started to drizzle as sympathetic hands helped him load Maria's cases into his car while she was carefully transferred to the ambulance. By then the police had arrived and began taking statements and John had difficulty getting permission to leave. He was still without his jacket and he was wet through by the time he quoted Jamieson's name and they reluctantly let him drive off towards the hospital.

'But we'll want to speak to you later.'

At the hospital he gave the people at the reception desk as many details as he could while Maria was whisked away. Her name, that she was a visitor to this country, and no, he didn't know of any relatives . . . and all the time he was numb with shock. For an instant it hadn't been Maria lying on the pavement, but his wife Trish, who had the same colour of hair, the same build.

He hadn't been a witness to his wife's death but he'd heard all the details at the inquest and he'd had to imagine what

the scene was like, with the drunk driver crying and saying he
was sorry. David, only four weeks old, had been miraculously
safe in his pram . . . And now it had all been transferred in
time and he was seeing it for real, seven years later.

Maria had been taken behind the green curtains of the
accident unit before he got to the hospital and he had to sit
in an overheated waiting-room. After a while his damp
clothes began to steam. He waited patiently, knowing that
someone would come eventually to tell him if she was still
alive. There were others waiting with the same anxious
expressions, but no one spoke to anyone else. One woman
had a young child with her who got fractious, cried for a
drink, and the continual grizzling got on everyone's nerves
until finally someone went in search of a drinks machine.

And John began to think clearly. The snatches of conversation came back, especially the witness who had angrily
said that the car had 'mowed' Maria down. That kept going
through his mind. A drunk had done the same to his wife,
mounted the pavement where she was pushing David in his
pram, but although it had been a criminal act it had not
been deliberate as the witness was claiming that this had
been. Maybe the driver had in fact been drunk when he
lost control and hit Maria . . .

An hour passed and the initial urgency with which they'd
taken Maria away seemed to have abated. The doctors and
nurses were still with her and she must still be alive or they
would have come to tell him, surely?

He walked along the corridor and waited until a nurse
appeared.

'Can you tell me what's happening to Maria Twarog?'

'Are you a relative?' She was already edging away to deal
with other emergencies.

'No, but I'm the nearest you'll get to one. There isn't
anyone else.'

'I'll ask,' she said. 'I'll get someone to come to the
waiting-room to see you as soon as we know what her condition is.'

The police arrived; two constables who had been at the

LEGACY   79

scene who recognized John. 'What can you tell us, Mr
Leith?'
He explained that Maria was a visitor to the city and
that he was a friend. Yes, he'd been going to pick her up
but the accident had already happened when he arrived.
No, he hadn't seen how it happened.
'One of the people there said the driver went up on the
pavement,' he said, in case they hadn't been told, but one
of them nodded.
'Yes, a few said that, but someone noticed a cat in the
road, so the driver could have swerved, lost control momen-
tarily—it happens.'
'Have you found him?
'We don't know it's a "him", but no, we haven't any
clues. It happened close to the corner and the car was into
the main stream of traffic before anyone could think of
taking the number. The best we got was that it was large
and grey—most of them agreed on that. One said possibly
a Volvo. We'll circulate all the garages to watch out for
damage. Any word on the girl yet?'
'I've just asked—the nurse is going to find out.'
At that moment a doctor appeared. 'Who's with Miss
Twarog?'
They all went into the corridor; one of the policemen was
poised to take notes.
'We're not sure how bad it is yet. She's in X-ray at the
moment, then she may need to go to theatre, or she may
be transferred to the Western. Looks as if the head injury
is the worst.'
'Serious?' a policeman asked.
'Oh yes. We need a relative, but I understand she's a
tourist.'
'From Canada, and I've never heard her mention any
relatives,' John said. 'I have her address back at the office,
I'll see what I can find out.'
'Well, I should do that. You won't be able to see her for
a while anyway.'
The mother and small girl came out of the waiting-room

and John stood aside to let her past. The woman was smiling. She'd got good news anyway.

It was good to get outside even though the fog had not lifted and was now an enveloping damp blanket. It was still raining as well, icy droplets that soaked his newly dried clothes as he headed for his car. He was thoroughly chilled as he drove back to Kramer's, only to find that Tollis was out. No one was sure when he would be back, so he went up to his own office and began a long stint on the phone, trying to trace someone related to Maria.

It took some time but eventually the phone rang in her home in Canada, but there was no answer. If anyone else lived there they might be at work, so he contacted the Canadian police. Yes, they would do their best to help but it might take some time.

Time was something he didn't want hanging heavy on his hands. Then he remembered Maria's luggage. Would there be anything in the cases that would give a clue to her relatives? He went down to his car and carried them up to his flat, then stood looking down at the evidence that the car had hit them with force. He would have to break the locks and it seemed an intrusion. In the end he decided to wait to see how urgently the information was needed, and stowed the cases in the bedroom.

The Canadian police worked quickly but the news was not good. Neighbours told them that Maria had lived with her mother, now deceased, and since they were immigrants the only relations were likely to be still in Poland. John phoned the hospital, heard that Maria had indeed been transferred to the Western and called there next to tell them what he had found out.

'How is she?'

'She's in the theatre now and it will be some time before we have anything definite to report,' the doctor told him.

It was his turn to be preoccupied that evening. In the end he told Clare what had happened and she guessed immediately that it had brought back painful memories.

'Oh God, how awful,' was all she said.

'The police are considering whether or not it was an accident.'

'What else could it be?'

John shrugged. 'One of the bystanders was convinced the driver aimed the car at her.' He got up and paced the floor. 'It sounded so convincing—there was no doubt in that man's mind that the driver ran her down—but why, for Christ's sake? She's a nice kid, here on the first proper holiday of her life. She hasn't had time to make an enemy.'

Clare was still. 'Of course she hasn't,' she said. 'Witnesses always have ten different versions of what happens in an accident. And speaking of accidents—that was not a bump you got from slipping, was it?'

He dropped down beside her and slipped an arm around her shoulders. 'No. I got thumped by a biker. I didn't want you worrying.'

'But I did anyway. Are you always going to get mixed up with Sentinel's affairs?'

It was calmly asked but he didn't doubt the importance of it. Clare wanted the whole truth this time and he gave it.

'I'm not going to work full time for Sentinel, but I might get involved sometimes. I see Tollis every day and I get a sniff of something, get intrigued . . .'

'You must have been crossed with a bloodhound,' she said with mock seriousness. Then she sighed. 'As long as I know.'

'It doesn't mean that there is always going to be trouble. I wouldn't mind having a go at the routine things as well. But if it worries you . . .'

'I just want to know what you are doing. We're not married but we have a "for better, for worse" sort of thing don't we? I don't want to be kept in the dark.' She was tense as she spoke and he knew that it had been on her mind a lot lately.

'I'll give it up,' he said, but she drew away and turned her head to look directly into his eyes.

'That wouldn't be a recipe for a happy future, would it? I tell myself that the other men who work for Sentinel are married and their wives must worry too, but I don't know if can take it, John. Doesn't the violent side scare you at all?'

He thought about the biker, the threats, and knew that he was no hero figure. The man did scare him, but it didn't stop him wanting to identify him. 'I won't be warned off, if that's what you mean. That's how I am,' he said simply, hoping she would understand.

She leaned against him and was silent for a bit. Then he felt her body relax. 'I suppose it could be worse,' she said lightly. And he could see that she was trying very hard to recapture the easy atmosphere they usually enjoyed. 'After all, you might be uninterested in sex . . .'

'Never.'

She smiled under his lips. 'Prove it.'

It was playful banter, but they both understood what had happened. Clare had needed to know how he felt about working with Tollis and at the back of her mind was the night that she'd been shot. She was trying to come to terms with it, but he was under no illusion that the problem was going to just disappear. Face it, deal with it, was her philosophy on everything, but this time that wasn't so easy and it was making her unhappy.

'I will give up working with Tollis if that's what you want,' he murmured later as they lay in bed. Clare looked troubled and shook her head.

'It's not the answer,' she said. 'I'd lose you eventually.'

And she was still struggling with it in the morning. Although she tried to hide it, he could tell that there was an inner argument going on inside her and there was nothing he could do to help her make the decision. He'd meant what he said about keeping away from Sentinel but wasn't sure if she believed he could do it.

He phoned the hospital before he left, feeling the signs of

a cold coming on, and by the time he'd been put through to the ward he was sneezing.

'Her condition is serious,' the sister said. 'No, no visitors yet. We've had to tell another caller the same thing—a cousin I believe. He was quite annoyed, but really there's nothing we can tell him for the moment.'

'Did he give his name? The police are anxious to trace friends or relatives.'

'No, he didn't and we don't ask.'

John put the phone down thoughtfully. A cousin? Why not, there might be Scottish relations from Lucy's side of the family?

Tollis had already left by the time he reached Kramer House so he left a short note about Maria on his desk. The meeting was due to start at ten in the large conference room and Val had come dressed for the occasion in a businesslike suit and a blouse with a frill at the neck.

'How many are we expecting?'

'Six.' She spoke shortly. 'Can I ask if I'm attending as your assistant or not?'

'Not. Sorry, I should have made that clear. You'll take a place with everyone else and we'll need a secretary along to take notes. You'll be free to speak on equal terms.'

'I intend to,' she said.

He was not looking forward to this, he told himself as he made his way to the meeting. He was stepping into Rees's shoes and tying up the laces, committing himself to the future of Kramer's. Part of him didn't want it, but part of him was also feeling that it wasn't so bad, not if he could get Kramer's organized in such a way that he could still have some free time to work with Tollis. Then a wave of guilt swept over him as he remembered how Clare felt about it. Maybe she was right. It wouldn't be easy to be tied to a desk permanently.

CHAPTER 7

'The meeting started off better than I expected,' he told Tollis later that afternoon. 'I think they were a bit put out that I haven't yet named a general manager—it's far too soon for that. But they perked up when I mentioned Ian Lambert's idea for giving the directors share options. It was when I asked them to offer suggestions that it fell apart. That was when Val stood up and said the business was too scattered. She suggested moving all the offices into that vacant property in George Street. Apparently it is large enough to take a slimmed down business and has a more prestigious address . . . She jumped the gun and they didn't like it, especially since she was hinting at redundancies. Why the hell couldn't she wait?' He saw that Tollis looked troubled.

'Sorry. It's not your business. But the whole thing blew up in her face; the resentment that she was there in the first place. They didn't see her as a director and it got a bit tense.'

'How tense?'

John grimaced. 'I didn't know that she had a child. Someone hinted that if there was an emergency her status as mother would come first because it has in the past.'

'And does it make a difference?'

'Of course not, but it was the way Val handled the meeting that worried me.' He could see that Tollis was angry but there was no outburst as he'd expected. In fact he didn't look all that surprised.

'She's had a bad time,' Tollis said at last. 'I could have told you, but it was up to Val . . . Her husband walked out when the boy was diagnosed as having Down's syndrome. He's ten now and Val's over-protective and she pays for a resident carer-cum-nanny. That's what the crisis was—the woman left without giving notice.'

'Can't he go to school?'

Tollis shrugged. 'That's what I've often suggested. He's bright and he needs company but she won't hear of it. Sometimes I think . . . Well, never mind what I think. It takes all she earns to pay for specialist care. She doesn't have room in her life for anyone else—I found that out a long time ago.'

Tollis looked directly at John and spoke without rancour. 'Her son and her job are all she cares about, and I'm not sure it works out best for the boy—so your new directors already had some ammunition because she does put her son first. But it sounds like they were making use of it.'

He frowned. 'And there's something else that may be affecting her judgement. Her ex-husband contacted her recently for some reason and she's edgy.'

'Mm.' John drew his hands wearily across his face and wondered what other problems he'd face before things were settled. 'Did you get my message about Maria?'

He gave Tollis more details of what had happened. 'So until the police find the driver, they're keeping an open mind about whether it was an accident or not.'

'Did you let Smith know? I suppose as her lawyer he should be told, so he can protect her interests. The driver will probably be traced and Maria will get damages.'

'I've been putting if off.'

'It's your case—she chose you. Do what you think is best. How's the Bridie McGuire thing going?'

'I'm waiting to hear about old schoolfriends, or anyone who might know where she is. Can I use Sentinel's resources, if I need them?'

'As long as you don't ask for manpower. Mike's the exception—he can be spared, if you can get hold of him. He's so bloody unpredictable at the moment and I haven't seen him for a day or so.'

'I take it that business is picking up?'

'I'm snowed under. All the men are on overtime. It happens,' he said. 'And you look as if you've got 'flu.'

John had been sneezing all day and his head felt as if it was floating. 'Just a cold,' he said.

John phoned Smith's office from his own room but he had to leave a message about Maria's accident with Smith's secretary because the lawyer was with a client.

He glanced at his watch and decided to pay a visit to the Western. He wasn't sure if he would be allowed to see her, but at least he might be able to speak to the sister in charge.

He was asked to wait until someone could speak to him and he took a seat beside the relatives of other patients who all looked anxious.

'Mr Leith?' The sister was Irish, soft-spoken, had curly red hair. 'I'll take you along to the door so that you can look in.' As they walked she gave him the report. 'The surgeon has relieved the pressure on Maria's brain. She needs a ventilator still but her condition is stable. We have to wait and see now.'

Then he was looking into the room where Maria lay. She looked as if she was in a deep sleep, but with her head bandaged and a tube running into her nose, another into a vein in the back of her hand, it had to be more than sleep that was keeping her eyes closed. She was pale, fragile, and surrounded by equipment; monitors and a pump to give her artificial respiration via the tube in her nose. A nurse was in the room with her.

'It's all so technical,' John said.

'Think of it as giving the body a rest—the machines take over for a bit—until the body is strong enough to function by itself.'

'Will there be any permanent damage to her brain?'

'There has been some damage but we don't know how badly it will affect Maria. Hopefully not too much. So far so good.'

Poor girl, he thought. She'd been so happy, so eager for the rest of her holiday. Idly he wondered how much she had inherited . . . enough to support her if her injuries left some disability? What an end to a holiday. And as he left the hospital and returned to Kramer House, he hoped the police would find the hit-and-run driver and that he was made to cough up for what he'd done.

As soon as he was in his own office he dialled Mrs McGuire's number.

'Just checking to see if you remembered any of Bridie's old schoolfriends.'

'I did remember one but she hasn't seen my daughter for ages.'

'I'd like to go and see her. I may be able to jog her memory and get the names of some other schoolfriends from her and she'll have had time to think about it now.'

'I wrote it down somewhere.'

John waited while she searched, heard the sound of the television in the background, a quiz show. Then she was back and he took note of a Christine Anderson's address. It was 5.45 p.m. The new contact might now be home from work and if he was lucky he'd catch her before she went out again. A personal visit might also be wiser than a phone call.

The tail-enders of the office staff were leaving for the day as he went down the stairs and even Sentinel was in darkness. Only the doorman was in the reception area, patiently waiting to check the lingerers out. He would hand over to the night man at 10.0 p.m. Three men worked three shifts of eight hours each and John knew them all by sight now that he used the top floor flat regularly. The men were necessary since the Sentinel entrance was not locked at night because the Sentinel employees came and went at all hours, either to consult or to pick up equipment.

It was quite dark when John went around the back to the parking area but for security reasons it was well lit, with a floodlight on the wall of the building. In any case, he was becoming used to travelling quickly between points of safety; out of the office and into his car, or sticking with crowds when he was out on the street.

The girl he was going to see was the same age as Bridie and lived in a flat in the student area of Bruntsfield,

according to the address Mrs McGuire had given him. He
found the street on the edge of Bruntsfield Links, one of
the many green areas that were dotted all over the city.
Normally, he would have walked there but that might be
exactly what the biker was hoping he would do. John
accepted that they were playing an adult version of hide-
and-seek now, with the seeker determined to prevent him
from finding Bridie. The man had to be a fruitcake to get
so worked up about the prospect of losing the proceeds of
a few burglaries, and that was the worrying factor. Did he
intend real harm or had the gesture with the imaginary gun
been only a threat, meant to scare him?

He let his mind probe other possibilities as he drove.
Jamieson was concerned for Bridie's safety and she had
been silent for some days.

'Let's hope you've left town and that you're safe,' John
murmured as he cruised slowly up the street where Christine Anderson lived. He tried to see the door numbers of
the tall blocks and when he found the one he was looking
for, he sat in the car for a bit to make sure that no one had
followed him. Then he looked over at the entrance to the
flats, to the path with high hedges on both sides. The front
door stood wide open and the close was well lit, showing
the stone staircase leading upwards. Going in would be no
problem but coming out again would be a different matter
and he wished that he'd not used the recognizable Granada.

He had to move, get in there and see if the girl could
help with more names, but leaving the car had to be on a
par with a turtle leaving its shell. Sighing, he stepped into
the night.

'Yes, I knew Bridie, but I told her mother that I've not
seen her for ages.'

They were in a large sitting-room that was littered with
magazines, cassettes, clothing and the remains of a meal.
There was no place to sit, so John remained standing while
Christine's two flatmates sat on the floor. They were

attending to each other's hair and make-up and openly listening at the same time.

'We're going out soon,' she explained. 'In ten minutes,' she added meaningfully.

'I know what you told Bridie's mother, but I hoped you'd know of some other of her classmates from school.'

'What's she done anyway?' She was curious but she was also suspicious of John.

'She hasn't been at work and her mother's anxious.'

'Yeah, well, she was always too quiet, if you see what I mean.' She looked at her watch and shrugged. 'I've got an old address book somewhere but I can't look for it now.'

'I could give you all a lift to where you're going if that would help,' John said.

The three girls conferred and Christine nodded. 'OK.' She strolled into a bedroom and left the door wide enough for John to see that if anything it was more untidy than the room he was in.

The next ten minutes were a revelation and he was soon wishing that Christine would hurry back. He was not used to being discussed as if he wasn't there.

'He's like Terence Stamp,' one said, but the other scoffed.

'He's too tall, too young.' She agreed there was a similarity, though, especially the eyes. He was relieved when the importance of making themselves ready to go out made them lose interest in him. One girl held a long gold earring up against the lobe of her ear and her friend nodded approval. He could hear drawers being pulled out in the bedroom and at last Christine appeared.

'Here's the address book,' she said, handing it over. 'Send it back when you're finished with it. You could try most of the names in there.'

They left the building together, with the girls clicking down the stairs in front of him in very high heels, mini skirts, endless legs in black tights and earrings reaching their shoulders. There was no biker in sight waiting for his exit. He dropped the girls off at a piano bar, refused a laughing invitation to join them, and drove back to Kramer's to study the addresses.

Tollis was still out, he noticed as he went up to the flat, but when he got there he saw that the door was slightly ajar. There was no light coming from inside the flat and no sound either. He pushed the door open gently and let it swing all the way back against the wall, then reached to the hallstand for a walking stick that had belonged to Rees. It clattered against the wood of the stand as he withdrew it and he froze, listening for a reaction from inside. Nothing. Just a faint smattering of rain against a window, a car horn from the street below. He reached for the light switch and flattened himself against the wall as the hallway was flooded with light. With his nerve endings tingling, he pushed open all the doors leading off the hall. The flat was empty.

Someone had been in there, though. Maria Twarog's cases had been forced open and her belongings emptied out on the floor. He stood in the doorway for a few moments and then left everything where it was and ran down the stairs to look for the doorman.

'I can't be out front every second,' the man protested. 'I can hear the door opening, but I've always said it should be locked and anyone wanting to get in could ring the bell. I was probably making my tea,' he went on defiantly. 'I am allowed tea-breaks, you know.'

'So you didn't see anyone?'

The man sighed. 'I didn't say that. Mr Tollis was in for a bit and two others went upstairs but I know both of them by sight.'

'Did Tollis say where he would be?'

'He leaves a number. It's in my room,' the man said. He was upset and John tried to pacify him.

'It's not your fault.'

The man still mumbled while John looked at the message Tollis had left, that only urgent calls should be relayed. How urgent was urgent? He decided that Tollis would classify this one as part of John's case and that he would have to deal with it himself. The question of strangers gaining admittance to the building was something else.

From his bedroom doorway he saw that Maria's clothes had been dumped in heaps from the two suitcases but the most attention had been given to a holdall. Documents, including her passport and return air tickets, a wallet and various other pieces of paper were stacked neatly, as if the intruder had gone through them carefully. The trouble was that John didn't know if any were now missing and Maria was in no condition to supply the answers.

He sat on the edge of the bed and pondered. What was so important that the man had risked entering the building where he could be spotted? It changed everything. It cast doubt on whether the hit-and-run had been an accident for a start.

He phoned the number where he could usually leave a message for Jamieson and was told he was off duty but that the message would be relayed to him.

'I'll come,' the Chief Inspector said when he phoned back. The call had been put through to him at home where he'd been watching a film on television, but he didn't sound put out by the interruption.

'Your calls are always so interesting,' he explained later when he viewed the disturbed bedroom. 'Did you touch anything?'

John shook his head.

'Right then, we'll have our little chat in the other room and let the experts discover if our friend wore gloves. He probably did, but they can dust the place in case he was careless.' Jamieson had come in casual clothes, a polo shirt under a cable-knit cardigan which had wooden buttons. It dipped at the front as if he made good use of the pockets, but even so, he still looked well groomed.

'From the start, Mr Leith,' he said, settling into a chair, and as John explained where he'd been that evening, Jamieson interrupted.

'Why spend your free time looking for that girl?'

That led to more explanations about the man on the

motorbike and the threats he'd made. Jamieson frowned.

'Carry on,' he said with a wave of his hand, wanting the whole picture before he commented on parts of the story. So John explained about his involvement with Maria and then about her accident.

'I heard about that, but another officer is handling it.'

'Have you found the driver?'

'Don't think so, but garages will have been circulated to look out for damage to a car—the investigating team will have an idea of the sort of damage it is likely to show.' Jamieson leaned forward. 'But you know, if the driver were to shut the car away, they might never find him.'

'Not many people could afford to do that, though, could they? You can't just go out and replace a car.'

'Exactly. So hopefully he'll use it and someone will notice —neighbours are often the ones to ask questions. "Had a bump?" they say and then they hear about the police inquiry. I suppose that after this—' he waved in the direction of the bedroom—'you're beginning to doubt that it was an accident.'

'I've been thinking about it, but—if the witness was right and the man deliberately ran Maria down, he wasn't around to see me take her luggage. How would he know it was here?'

Jamieson looked pleased. 'I'm glad you are thinking and not just jumping to conclusions. All the same, I'm prepared to keep an open mind because why would anyone want to come here to look through her suitcases—unless he was a chancer who thought the cases were yours—and that doesn't jell either, does it?'

'Surely the two incidents must be linked,' John said eagerly, but Jamieson smiled and shook his head.

'You can always construct a sinister meaning from scraps of evidence, but there can be another answer when bits of the jigsaw are missing.'

'Tell me one,' John said vehemently.

'All right. Let's say that the driver lost control, hit the girl and then drove off in fright. Now the man is dithering about coming forward. Then we have a separate situation; Bridie McGuire, equally scared and being looked for by a man who rides a motorbike. He decides that you have a clue to where she is and he brazenly walks in here to search your bedroom. Maria's clothes could be mistaken for Bridie's. Only when he sees the passport does he realize his mistake. Does that also sound possible?'

John had to agree that it did.

'So, we proceed with what we have. Is Maria Twarog able to answer questions?'

'She's still unconscious.'

'Then we look for Bridie and the man on the motorbike and the men who are breaking into empty houses. When we can't proceed in a direct line we work on the side-shoots until we can bring them all together. Sherlock Holmes said something like that . . .' Jamieson stood up and thrust his hands into the pockets of his cardigan. 'I can't stand the man but he did have his moments. He said "When all else is ruled out, what is left must be the truth"—or something like that.' He moved to the door. 'Patience, but be careful that your natural curiosity doesn't get you into more trouble.'

'Are you any closer to catching the burglars?'

'We know from what they took that they don't know what to look for, so there was no one writing a shopping-list for them. They left some good stuff lying around, so that sets their status in the criminal scale of things. What sort of work did Bridie do, by the way?'

'She keyed in information about properties for our computer records. Any copy typist could have done it.'

Jamieson seemed to have something more on his mind. 'She doesn't strike me as being very bright—not the type to think up a scheme like this. She could have met one of the men socially, I suppose, but according to her mother and her friends, she didn't go out. So I can't help wondering how the two came together, the shy girl and the boyfriend who likes to steal.'

John waited while Jamieson thought aloud.

'Is it possible that someone else in your offices planted the seed? We were talking about alternative scenarios for Maria and we could do the same for Bridie, couldn't we? Someone cleverer than Bridie sees the chance to make a bit of money on the side, contrives to introduce the criminal to a plain little girl who craves romance and excitement . . .' Jamieson chuckled. 'You aren't the only one with an imagination,' he said before he left.

John thought over what the policeman had said, especially about someone else from the office being involved. Just for a moment his subconscious took over and he remembered the remark Tollis had made about Val, how she had the expense of paying for specialist care for her son. There was also her mood of late, her short temper, and the way she'd acted out of character at the meeting . . . But he couldn't see her coldly picking Bridie to act as a scapegoat. That was patently ridiculous. He went to bed feeling totally confused all the same.

CHAPTER 8

If anything, his cold was worse in the morning, and to add to his discomfort Tollis seemed more concerned that someone had been free to wander around Kramer House than in anything to do with the Maria Twarog case. He was leaving John strictly on his own, in a sort of proving ground, to find out for himself that he was expected to use his own judgement, to follow up any piece of evidence— and to look after himself.

'Jamieson spoke to the doorman after he left you last night,' Tollis said. 'He questioned him about the two men who had been in, and from the descriptions he gave, one of them certainly doesn't work for me, but the doorman insists that he knows him. You might speak to him and see if it could have been one of your people who was in—just to eliminate him if nothing else. You won't see the doorman until he comes back on duty, though.'

Someone who worked for Kramer's? It fitted in with the suggestion Jamieson had made, but who? In the meantime, he decided to take Jamieson's advice and concentrate on finding Bridie McGuire and the man on the motorbike. There was nothing he could do for Maria until—hopefully —she came out of her coma and was able to answer questions.

He studied the notebook that Christine Anderson had given him. There were a great many names scrawled in it but he narrowed them down to those she had earmarked for Christmas cards, assuming them to be close friends. He also assumed that all of them were the same age group and therefore likely to be out at work or furthering their education, so he postponed contacting them until later in the evening.

He sneezed again and went in search of Val, coffee and aspirins.

'You should have stayed in bed,' she said, dropping a couple of tablets into a glass and then giving it a swirl. 'The staff has been decimated by this 'flu virus.'

'I've only got a cold,' he said.

Val shrugged, as if she had little sympathy to spare and he remembered with guilt the small niggle of doubt he'd had about her the night before. If she had personal troubles with an ex-husband on the scene, that would account for her mood and she was not the type to share confidences.

'I'll be out for a few hours,' he said, draining the last of the coffee. 'And the next week is going to be unpredictable.'

'I can manage,' she said, smiling.

She would. Publicly and privately.

He phoned Garek just before lunch. 'Any word on the motorbike?' He wondered if Garek had made any attempt to trace the owner or if it had been an empty promise.

'I'm going to see someone this afternoon,' Garek said. 'Would you like to come along to find out for yourself?'

'Sure, where are we going?'

'To look at a list of HOG members—Harley Owners Group—HOG Caledonia to be exact.'

'Sounds interesting,' John said, and his hopes suddenly soared. They might discover the identity of the owner of the Harley which had begun to haunt his dreams, but Garek interrupted his euphoria.

'If you like—' he paused—'I could take you on one of my machines.' He had spoken hesitantly and John detected something unusual, rare, in the man's voice. Garek was offering a shared pleasure in something that was his own private passion. Garek, who had always been coldly aloof, always defensive to the point of violence as far as Albert Gumley was concerned, had a soft spot after all and he was allowing John a very small glimpse of it. The wrong answer now would bring the portcullis clanging down forever.

'I'd be . . .' He searched for the right word. 'Honoured' would be condescending, 'delighted', over the top. 'I'd like that very much,' he said and Garek made the arrangements stiffly. John was to drive to Gumley's house and they would leave from there. And he could sense from Garek's tone that the man was looking forward to showing him his collection of treasures.

The aspirin had done nothing to clear the thick feeling in his head and he set off for Cramond, where Gumley had his house, with eyes that ached from the dazzle of the late winter sunshine. It should be spring, but it wasn't yet. It was very cold—or was that the feverish shivering of early 'flu? He turned on the heater and then realized that he had chosen the wrong route as he saw the traffic moving slowly ahead of him.

Queensferry Road was jammed with double lines of cars, buses and lorries, all inching along in the same direction, no doubt because of road works ahead. It was the same every day in the morning and evening rush hours as the commuters headed for the Forth Bridge but he hadn't expected it at lunch-time. He fumed, knowing he could have done the journey quicker by taking the roundabout route along the coast.

For half an hour he made little progress and he could have used the time to plan ahead—what to do if they managed to identify the biker—but he was drowsy and couldn't think clearly. He opened a window, but that just introduced exhaust fumes into the car and even when he shut it, the smell lingered. He had skipped lunch in his eagerness to meet Garek and now he felt the beginnings of nausea. He should have listened to Val and gone back to bed . . .

'Christ, give yourself a shake,' he muttered, angry with himself, and reached to switch on some music. But it was one of Clare's cassettes, something by Vivaldi that was one of her favourites, when what he really needed to wake him up were the gravelly tones of Dave Lee Roth. His mind wandered. Strange how different their tastes were in music, yet they were compatible in everything else, especially in bed.

He was finding if difficult to concentrate and once his foot slipped off the gas pedal. His limbs felt heavy, his hands were tired holding the wheel. It had to be 'flu, but he'd see Garek as arranged and then go home to sweat it out.

He hadn't noticed that a long gap had developed between him and the car in front and angry hoots came from behind, urging him to move up while he had the chance or to let someone else fill the gap. It took all his concentration to join up his random thoughts about Clare, Garek, the need to steer the car ahead. When the jam suddenly eased and the vehicles in front of him accelerated, it took him unawares again, and his reactions were dreamlike. A taxi drew up to his bumper and he saw the driver's impatient expression in his mirror. The man was swearing, waving a fist. A fuss about nothing, was John's languid thought as he felt his foot slide off the gas pedal yet again.

'Oops,' he said aloud. Then he had difficulty lifting his foot back on. His shoe weighed a ton, the muscles of his leg protested when asked to lift the weight. The taxi-driver was mouthing more swear words when at last he got moving again and then, just ahead, John saw a right turn that would take him out of the flow of traffic.

He almost missed it. His hands tried to turn the wheel but it seemed incredibly heavy and he went forward so slowly that he nearly landed on the opposite pavement. Maybe he should stop and stretch his legs, gulp in some fresh air, he thought, but he had only a short distance to go . . .

He screwed his eyes shut for an instant and then opened them wide, wondering in a brief lucid moment if Val had given him a patent 'flu remedy that forbade driving. Maybe she'd missed the small print on the label. Too late now, he mused, fearlessly taking the side road at . . . he glanced down at the speedometer and saw that he was doing a cautious twenty-eight miles an hour. Yet it seemed too fast. The lamp posts on the kerbside were whizzing up to him and he began to count them, like milestones, to try to stop sleep taking over.

He was too muddled to think clearly. There was something very wrong with his brain. He was aware of it but the reason evaded him. It was like being on the edge of sleep, in that half-conscious state when random thoughts led to dreams, where the warmth of the duvet spread slowly through cold limbs, where he was a second or two from sliding into deep, deep slumber.

Just ahead he saw the gates of Gumley's home standing open. The car passed through them, scraping a wing on a stone pillar, and then the wheels hit the gravel of the drive. The chip-stones were bright pink and they stretched up around a long bend to the house itself. He had never noticed how clean they were before and wondered if Gumley had the men wash them. The car moved slower than ever, with the wheels apparently sinking into the stones, as if they were quicksand. John felt laughter rise up in his chest like the bubbles in champagne. He was driving into a man trap set by his malevolent father-in-law, a deep pit of chip-stones.

Pity Clare wasn't here to share the joke, but she was off

to London, or was she? He saw the tree slowly looming in front of him but was powerless to avoid it and when the car hit it, it was with a gentle bump. Then he sighed with relief because he didn't have to go any further, and he laid his head down on the wheel and closed his eyes.

He woke to waves of nausea, in a cold sweat, lying on Gumley's cream-covered sofa. Garek was leaning over him, holding something firmly against his face. His bald head and pallid skin looked like a giant egg.

'Take deep breaths,' he said and John obeyed, feeling instant improvement, as if someone was pulling wads of cotton wool out of his head. Then he became aware that he was breathing in oxygen and that Garek was holding the mask on his face, Gumley's mask. He reached up to push it away, as if it was contaminated.

'I'm all right,' he said with a tongue that felt like rubber. Garek looked doubtful but he didn't argue, nor did he help John to sit up, but wheeled the oxygen cylinder back to stand in its usual place beside Gumley's chair. John followed him with his eyes and saw that Gumley was watching him with an expression of pure pleasure. John eased himself into a sitting position and swung his heavy legs to the floor. He was very weak, uncoordinated. His hands didn't quite go where he wanted them to go and his brain still wasn't functioning properly. He couldn't remember getting to the house, or why he was there.

Garek forestalled any questions by asking one of his own. 'Your car was full of exhaust fumes—why didn't you smell them?'

'I did, faintly, but I thought it was the heavy traffic— and I'm all bunged up with a cold.' Then what Garek had said really sank in. Carbon monoxide. 'I felt sleepy.'

'You were not sleeping when I pulled you from the car. You were almost unconscious. You hit the pillar at the gate and then ran into a tree.'

'Don't remember,' John mumbled. It was tiring to try to work it out and then sweat broke out for real as he realized how dangerous he'd been on the road, to himself and everyone else. 'There must be something wrong with the car.'

'I will get our man to look it over,' Garek said. 'You must be still and not try to move yet.' Then he headed for the door.

And John knew that Garek was right because his body very definitely didn't want to move. He was left alone with Gumley and he could see that the old man was enjoying the situation. It had made his day, might even prolong his life-expectancy.

'You could have stalled under the wheels of a container truck,' Gumley said. 'And then I would have outlived you. Life is so unpredictable.' He shook his head wonderingly and his skeletal fingers pleated the blanket that covered his knees. Enmity had become a way of life, a stimulant that was as good as any medical treatment. No doubt it was the only pleasure that the old man now had. John ignored him and presently Gumley's head drooped on his chest and he slept.

Garek and another man went by the window and John urged his weak limbs to support him so that he could watch what they were going to do. When he reached the window, Garek was standing beside the Granada and his companion was half under the car. The prostrate man handed something to Garek, who then strode quickly towards the house. John sat down again and waited to see what they had found.

'This is brake pipe,' Garek said, holding out a length of red tubing. 'My man says it is 3/16ths and that it was placed with one end in the silencer and the other going up through the floor following the wiring panel.'

Gumley had finished his catnap and was now demanding to know what was going on.

'I don't understand,' John said.

Garek spelled it out. 'There is nothing wrong with the car, this was deliberately inserted, through a hole in the silencer.'

John's thought processes were beginning to work again. Deliberately inserted, Garek had said, and it could only

have been done while it was parked behind the Kramer
building, probably after he drove back from Christine
Anderson's flat the evening before and maybe by the same
person who had tampered with Maria's luggage.

'If you had travelled a greater distance . . .'

'How difficult was it to fix?'

'Very simple.' Garek showed him how flexible the pipe
was. 'He would need a tool, a punch of some sort, to make
the hole in the silencer—he would not need to go far under
the car.'

'So he had to come prepared.'

'Yes, but not knowing if it would kill. There are too many
unknown elements, like how much you would inhale, if you
would open a window, if you would smell it—and the pipe
is so narrow, he was only guessing how much gas it would
carry into the car.'

'But he didn't care much about those variables, did he?
Whether I died, or killed anyone else,' John said bitterly.
'He didn't know I had a cold and couldn't smell the gas,
or that I would get stuck in traffic and have more time to
inhale it . . .'

Garek agreed with a nod. 'This man is the one you are
looking for?'

'The one who owns the Harley.'

'But I can't take you to look for him today. I will not
take you on my Fat Boy in case you fall off.'

'Fat Boy?'

Garek nodded solemnly. 'Come. Fresh air is good for
you. I will show you my Fat Boy, and the others.'

The air was cold but it was pure, sweet. John even welcomed the chill of it on his body and took deep gulps of it
as they walked across the gravel that now looked so very
ordinary. It crunched underfoot and shifted with each step
and he remembered clearly the illusion of the quicksand.
He would probably never tell anyone of the illusions caused
by the effects of the gas, but he would make the biker pay
in full one day soon.

Garek opened one of the garages with a remote-control

device and then stepped inside with John close on his heels. Several motorbikes were under shrouds, huge shapes that were slightly menacing until Garek threw a light switch. Then he reached out and pulled away the covers of one and revealed what lay underneath.

'Fat Boy,' he said, laying a hand on one wide handlebar. 'Weighs six hundred and fifty pounds, shotgun-style dual exhausts.' He said a lot more but John didn't take it in. The motorbike was enormous, beautiful, all chrome and gleaming black, a machine that even someone who was not an enthusiast would fall in love with. He walked around it, seeing how wide it was, the comfort of the leather seats, the steep angle of the front fork.

'Do you get the chance to ride it often?'

Garek shrugged. 'Not in town. If you park a machine like this you cannot get back to it. It gathers a crowd.' There was a laconic hint of pride in the words.

'What's the speed like?'

'About ninety. It is for comfort, touring, not speed.'

'Fat Boy,' John said. 'It's a good name.'

Garek had moved on. The next machine was just as special, but different in style and John suspected there was a bit of gamesmanship in the way Garek was revealing one at a time. He played along, feeling in a slightly unreal situation, still groggy. Looking over Garek's bikes was merely a diversion, but soon he would have to come to terms with the biker's intentions. Had the man followed him from the office and seen his erratic driving? Had he watched hopefully to see the Granada crash, be hit by another vehicle? What sort of bastard was he?

John realized he was supposed to be listening to what Garek was saying and gave the man his attention. There was no point in building up a head of steam until the biker was identified, then . . .

'. . . a Softtail Custom,' Garek was saying by way of introduction. Again there was the wide, raked-out fork in front, the chrome and leather.

'Comfortable,' Garek said, pointing to the soft seats.

'This is a buckhorn bar, set into the pullback risers . . .' He stopped when he saw that John looked interested but puzzled. 'It is why we join the HOG, so that we can talk Harleys. It becomes a way of life,' he said in an apologetic tone. 'Over there is a new Hugger, lower than the old model . . .'

'What model does our man have?'

'A sportster standard—maybe second-hand. There is a great turnover because only so many can be imported from the States. We should be able to trace him all the same.'

John felt his hopes sink. A second-hand bike might change hands many times. Garek saw his expression and was still hopeful.

'Those who buy them like to join the club.' He tried to explain further. 'It is special, to own any model. I will buy more.'

'Expensive hobby.'

Garek looked pained. 'I will never lose money on a Harley and it is not just a hobby.'

'Sorry.' He wanted to go with Garek now, to find the biker, but he still felt light-headed and knew that even if Garek offered to take him by car, it would be sensible to wait until another time. Besides, Garek wanted to take him on Fat Boy. 'Can we go tomorrow?'

'Yes. Now I will get one of the men to take you back to town.'

As they walked back to the house, John asked one more question because he was curious. 'Do you wear all the gear, the real Harley accessories?'

'Of course,' Garek said stiffly.

And that, John thought, would be something to see.

'You should see a doctor, you know,' Garek said. 'Although you appear to have recovered.' He closed the main door behind them and headed for a room that John had never been in before; it turned out to be a library and Garek knew exactly which book to reach for.

'I need medical knowledge sometimes, when Mr Gumley does not want doctors in the house. This is quite comprehensive.' He studied the index and then flicked through the pages sitting at a reading table, ignoring John completely.

After a time he looked up. 'It says here that carbon monoxide saturates the hæmoglobin in the blood and that sixty per cent is fatal. "There is rapid onset of muscular incoordination and weakness . . ." He checked that with John who nodded.

'Exactly how I felt, but I don't know about the percentages.'

'Obviously not. But we did the right thing by letting you rest. Exercise would have aggravated the symptoms.' He snapped the book shut, satisfied apparently that his nursing techniques were good. He was a very strange man indeed.

'And you appear to be well again. I will tell someone to get the car out for you and you will come back tomorrow to look for the man who tried to kill you.' He hesitated. 'Will you tell the police? I don't think Mr Gumley would like them inspecting your car in front of his house.'

'I'll take the brake pipe with me. I doubt if he left any other clues behind. Later I may tell Jamieson but I'd like to hand the man over to him at the same time. I'll get someone to collect the car.'

Garek seemed satisfied with that.

Carbon monoxide. A man on a Harley. Fat Boy. John repeated the words as he was chauffeured back to Kramer's.

CHAPTER 9

Garek's man dropped him close to the front door of Kramer House and John went directly to see Tollis. Most of the staff had already left, but there were one or two of Tollis's men in the outer office and their heads turned as he went by. They gave him no more than brief, curious glances because they had got used to seeing him around. No one seemed taken aback, so he assumed that he no longer looked

as bad as he felt. He was wrong. Tollis took one look and
came out from behind his desk.

'Christ, you look awful,' he said. He made no allowances
for the faint nausea that John still felt in the pit of his
stomach and demanded an immediate explanation.

John pulled the brake pipe from his pocket and outlined
what had happened. Tollis listened without interrupting
and then shook his head angrily.

'There's got to be more behind all this,' the big man
growled, staring at the red piece of pipe. It lay on the desk,
seemingly innocuous, and Tollis poked it with a finger. 'Got
to be,' he muttered. 'People kill when the stakes are high,
not to cover up some piddling burglaries . . . unless they're
mad. Your feelings about this are turning out to be right,
as usual; that we should have looked harder at both women,
the girl and . . . what was her name?'

'Mrs Pearson, guardian of the painting. I drew a blank
there, so I'm concentrating on Bridie.'

Tollis nodded that it was the right approach, still deep
in thought.

'How's Maria?'

'Not able to help us yet.'

Tollis looked him over. 'You still look bloody awful.
Would some food help?'

'Um, food doesn't sound a good idea at the moment.
Later, perhaps: I'll probably share Clare's supper.'

Tollis was still standing and now he moved his head in
a gesture that spelled bewilderment. 'You're taking this
calmly. Hasn't it hit you yet what might have happened?'

'I've been thinking of nothing else.'

'So what are you going to do? Jamieson will pull out all
the stops now—they've got to catch this bugger.'

'I'm so close to finding out who he is,' John murmured.
'Garek will ask around and he's confident that anyone who
owns a Harley will be easy to identify. I think Garek is
incensed that the biker will give the other Harley owners a
bad name.'

Tollis moved back behind his desk and dropped into his

chair. 'And in the meantime this joker will see you around. He'll try again.'

John nodded. He knew Tollis was right and that the best action he could take was to dump it all in the lap of the police and then hide himself somewhere safe. But he couldn't do it. Nor could he explain why, either to himself or to Tollis. It had something to do with not giving in to threats but at the same time he was scared. Scared that the man might dream up something even worse next time . . .

Tollis had been watching him. 'OK. I suppose I'd feel the same. Just don't take any chances—but I'm probably wasting my time telling you that.'

'I'm going to see that bastard in gaol,' John told him, standing up and trying not to look as if his legs were folding under him. 'And that means I have to find Bridie McGuire, so right now I'm going upstairs to phone her old schoolfriends.'

Tollis was still frowning as John shut the door behind him.

Going up the stairs, he found that his legs ached with the effort. No doubt some of the gas was still in his bloodstream, cutting the oxygen supply to his muscles. It was something he was familiar with, because a long race had the same effect. Prolonged exercise used up oxygen, and muscles suddenly began to tie up, making the finishing line seem an impossible target, but that was a normal process and not caused by a toxic gas. At that moment he wondered if he would ever feel like running again.

It was not to be a very fruitful evening as far as the search for Bridie was concerned. Some of the numbers he phoned were not answered, others said, 'Who?' as if Bridie had slipped from their memories. One girl said Bridie had been into yoga for a while and he could try the club to see if she was still a member.

He noted the name of the club and continued working his way through the list. If only Bridie had some interests —according to her mother she was not even a reader and had not joined a library. Was it possible to go through life and not be registered on paper somewhere?

'Yes, I remember her, we did a training course together,' another girl said and John brightened.

'What course was that?'

'Computers. She wasn't much good at it but I heard she landed a job.'

'Have you heard from her lately?' He held his breath.

'Last week. She turned up and asked for a bed—a cheek really, because I hadn't seen her for ages.'

'Last week. Do you know where she went after that?'

'Back home, I suppose. I thought maybe she'd had a row with her mother or something but she never said and I didn't ask. She would have told me the story of her life if I had—miserable little sod really.'

John put down the phone. Not only was Bridie not on any official record—not even for poll tax—but no one seemed to care. And she was only twenty. Her own fault to some degree? Possibly, having personality problems that she'd done nothing to improve, but for whatever the reason she had become one of life's outcasts and that made her a prime target. Someone had discovered Bridie's need to be liked and made use of her. Maybe she'd enjoyed it for a little while. He hoped so. It was just nine days since he'd first set eyes on the girl at the funeral and exactly a week since she'd last been in touch. Where the hell was she?

He didn't tell Clare about the booby-trap in the car or his intention to carry on despite it. They were in bed, had just finished the *Scotsman* crossword between them and were feeling smug about that, when he asked her opinion about Bridie.

'In her situation, where would you go?'

'I would have somewhere to go—she apparently hasn't. However, her boyfriend may have paid out her share of the loot and in that case I'd choose a nice hotel and spend the lot.' She turned on her side and put one bare leg over his. 'Your girl would pick somewhere quieter than a hotel because she wouldn't want people around, so maybe she'd rent a room. And she would be very frightened. I don't think she'll be quiet for much longer—she'll ask for help.'

'Go on.' Her cool reasoning sounded right; it fitted the Bridie he was beginning to know well.

Clare reached to switch off the light, edged closer.

'She doesn't feel comfortable with people and she has no confidence in herself either—she needs care and protection —from you or from her mum. So she'll reach the point where her need overcomes her fear. She'll phone somebody.'

'If only Jamieson could catch those two men. If the arrest was reported in the paper it might be just what she needs . . .'

'John.' It was no more than a whisper in his ear. 'She's not the only one who has needs.'

'And then I would be able to concentrate on Maria . . .'

Clare reached down and pinched his leg, hard.

'Ouch. So OK, OK, first things first . . .' He closed his mind to the events of the day, to his deliberate act of deceiving Clare, and let another stronger emotion take their place.

It was one of the best ways to make love, he was thinking while it was still in progress. Mouth on mouth to smother laughter, fumblings becoming caresses, and when the laughter died there was the serious business of prolonging the moments of passion. They knew each other's needs so well that their love-making was often begun in a casual, light-hearted way, but it soon became an exploration with no limits on time, no one to answer to, no one but themselves to consider. It was the most selfish of acts but one in which they were equal and willing partners.

They stayed close when it was over, clammy skin against clammy skin, lips still seeking with gentle kisses.

'I met a girl,' he murmured, 'who said I looked like Terence Stamp—except I'm taller and better-looking . . .'

She leaned away from him and he caught the gleam of her eyes in the dark. 'Where did you meet a girl? You don't look anything like him, but who was she?'

It wasn't important. It wasn't the moment to be drawn back to the business of Bridie McGuire and her friends. 'Nobody, just a girl. I'll tell you about it sometime.' He held her close until she slept and then lay awake for hours thinking that if the biker had succeeded that day, he would not have had this night with Clare, or any other night.

There was a postcard from David the next morning; a view of chalets from which the boys made their expeditions into the surrounding hills. It looked bleak enough to stiffen any boy's backbone—which was presumably what the boarding-school had in mind. He flipped it over and read the carefully rounded writing. *Dear Dad. The camp is great and so is the food. We walked ten miles today and tomorrow we are going canoeing. Love David.* Canoeing had been crossed out several times before he got it right. John propped the card up on his desk and spent the rest of the morning with Val, who was still looking pale and strained. He was tempted to probe a little, then decided that it was none of his business.

Instead he asked if she'd ever met Bridie.

'She helped out last summer when we were short of staff over the holidays—she usually works in the property management office, as you know.'

'What did you think of her?'

Val made a face. 'Well, she was quiet and not very bright. She had to be shown even routine things several times before she caught on, and to be honest, she wasn't much use. As a person, I didn't like her much.' Val thought a bit before going on. 'I don't mind shyness—it's understandable if rare these days, but that girl . . . there was a lot more under the surface, a sort of knowing look about her. Another woman would know what I mean,' she said with a shrug.

'Try me,' John said.

'To put it bluntly, she wanted a man. I think some of the men who met her sensed it. She was open to offers—and the other girls didn't like having her around.'

It cast a new light on the missing girl. She had been

persuaded to copy the lists, but maybe it hadn't taken much persuasion after all.

Just after eleven there was a call from Smith, inquiring about Maria.

'I should have rung you sooner. Terrible thing to happen,' Smith said. 'What's her condition? The hospital isn't very forthcoming.'

'I'll be going to see her later but as far as I know there's no change. It can take a while, apparently.'

'She's still unconscious, then?'

'There have been complications.'

'Ah. Let me know if there's anything I can do.'

'I will.'

John felt irritated as he hung up and at the same time knew there was no reason for it. Smith had got under his skin on that first meeting and that instant dislike was now colouring his assessment of the man's motives.

He had a snack lunch at his desk and set off to meet with Garek just before two, taking an anonymous car from the pool. To be sure of avoiding any hold-ups, he also took the longer coast road on what was turning out to be a real spring day. If the good weather lasted he faced a problem, because he'd planned to take Clare away for a couple of days as a birthday treat, perhaps to Elmwood. Now he would have to tell her it was cancelled, for until the biker was behind bars the trip was out of the question.

Garek was wearing a black leather jacket with the Harley logo on the back and he had a spare helmet laid out for John. The Fat Boy was parked in front of the garage, gleaming in the sunshine and looking more impressive than ever. It was not by any means a subtle style of bike; Garek probably wouldn't have owned it if it was.

'I was ready to take you,' Garek told him, 'but Mr Gumley is not well. Can you ride one of these?'

'I think so . . .' He couldn't believe that Garek was going to trust him with 10,000 quid's worth of Harley.

'Go to Alvin's. He's the only stockist in Scotland.' Garek

gave him the address as John put on the helmet. 'I'll phone
to let him know you're coming and he might point you in
the right direction. Even if the biker's machine is second-
hand someone will know its history.'

'What are our chances?'

Garek shrugged out of the jacket and passed it to John.
It was a perfect fit. 'We will find him, maybe not today,
but soon.' He sounded supremely confident.

The trip to the showroom didn't take long and for John
it was over too soon. Fat Boy had charisma, and was sheer
luxury to ride. It was like leaning back in a comfortable
armchair and he now believed what Garek had told him,
that it was possible to ride comfortably for ten hours on
such a machine. There was the feeling of sheer effortless
power in the engine that had a distinctive low rumbling
sound and he saw heads turning as he passed. Oh yes, it
would be easy to fall in love with a bike like this and he
now understood what Garek felt about his collection. It
could easily become a way of life, an obsession.

Inside the showroom there were dozens of bikes, some
more colourful than the ones Garek owned, but all distinctive in their own right. He walked around for a bit but the
manager must have been watching for him and soon he was
at John's elbow.

'Mr Leith?'

'Yes.' John let his fingers run over soft leather and reluctantly turned to face him. 'Did Mr Garek tell you what I
want to know?'

'Yes, and I've given it some thought. There are only
about thirty models like the one you are looking for—in
Edinburgh, that is—but I can narrow that down a bit.
Come into the office.'

The manager sat before a computer and while he
searched its records, John looked through the long glass
panel that overlooked the showroom. There were half a
dozen customers wandering among the bikes with the same
covetous expression he'd probably shown when he was
admiring the stock. There was even a familiar face, but he

couldn't place him. The man was at the accessories counter, side-on to John, dressed in a suit under a camel coat. He looked heavily prosperous, the sort of man who dined too well in the best places.

'There are about a dozen here that I can't put an owner to at the moment because they've changed hands,' the manager said, interrupting John's thoughts. 'But I can contact the most recent owners and try to track down the bikes if you like.'

'A dozen.' John was disappointed. 'How long will that take?'

'I can't say. It depends on how many times the bikes have been sold, but Mr Garek is a good customer . . . I'll do my best.'

Over his shoulder John saw that the man in the camel coat had turned round and was now looking at the bikes. His face was tantalizingly familiar, yet at the same time different, a bit rounder than he remembered and John frowned as he tried to place him. He was still staring when the other man glanced up and their eyes met. He was astonished to see shock registered in the other's eyes but it disappeared quickly and the eyes slid away. For a few more moments the man in the camel coat lingered, then walked quickly towards the door.

'Who's that?' John asked, but the manager had been bent over the desk and when he did look up the camel-coated man had gone.

'Excuse me, I must try to speak to him—I'll be in touch,' John said, hurrying from the office and dodging between the bikes to get to the door. He had parked Fat Boy just outside and as he reached it he looked around for the man, or for the car that he was in, but there was no sign of him. 'Damn.'

He got going, scouted the neighbouring streets, but he hadn't a hope in hell of spotting his quarry because he had no idea what sort of car he was driving. All the way back to Gumley's house he wondered about him—the man's expression had been so startled, as if John was the last person he'd expect to see in the place that sold Harleys. He'd more or less disappeared as soon as he spotted John, who was furious with himself because he had not moved quickly enough. His brain had just begun to tick over the possibilities, the remote chance that this man who obviously knew him by sight could be the one he was looking for, but his reactions had been far too slow. And by the time he was facing Garek he'd already had second thoughts.

'It couldn't have been him,' he said, shaking his head. 'He wasn't tall enough, was too fat and out of condition, but I wish I'd had the chance to speak to him all the same.'

They were in the sitting-room but Gumley's chair was empty. The fireplace was laid with paper and kindling but the fire had not been lit. Garek told him that Gumley had taken to his bed again.

'Not that there's any great change in his condition. What will you do now?' His features were set in their usual neutral expression but there was a glimmer of interest in his eyes.

'I feel as if I'm working with cobwebs,' John said. 'I touch a thread of information and try to follow it up but it never leads back to the centre of things. That man . . .' He shook his head with disappointment. 'I thought it was a break, that I'd actually come face to face with him at last. But he *was* startled when he saw me and he scampered out of there so fast . . . Why?' He looked at Garek and hoped he would agree it was a suspicious thing to do.

'Try to remember where you saw him last, and then ask him,' Garek said.

Garek always said the obvious and made it sound easy. 'I'll damn well try. At least it gives me something else to aim for.'

Garek, in his usual black trousers, matching waistcoat and white shirt, followed him to the door. 'What do you think of Fat Boy?' It sounded like an afterthought but in fact was a further lowering of Garek's defences. He was becoming almost friendly.

'Do you need to ask? I'm hooked. It's a great machine.

Maybe when this business is over . . .' He didn't need to
finish because Garek was already nodding.

'Any time,' he said.

And that meant he was welcome at Gumley's residence, by
Garek at least, and he'd never thought the day would come
when he would look forward to a return visit to his father-in-
law's home. The invitation had been genuine, but all the
same it was as well to bear in mind that Garek was Gumley's right hand and the wishes of the master always came
first.

The name of the man in the camel coat was bugging him.
Had he perhaps worked for Rees at some time? That was
a possibility, and there would be old staff records somewhere in the building but they would not include photographs. And John knew the man had changed since he last
saw him, was more corpulent for one thing. Would a verbal
description awake memories—with Tollis? The man's identity was lurking somewhere in the back of his mind but it
evaded him.

Tollis wasn't in and a phone call from Jamieson postponed further action.

'Aye, we got the two of them in the early hours, breaking
into a place up Colinton way. Would you like to come and
have a look at them? It would help us to know if you've
seen them hanging around.'

John headed for the police station where the two men
were being held. Things were beginning to move at last.

'Did you ask them about Bridie?'

'Yes, but they claim they don't know her. They're not
being entirely honest yet—they say they got the list of
properties from a man in a pub and I've heard that before.
However, they were caught red-handed and they've both
been done before for small jobs, so they know the ropes.
They'll open up. And I don't think you need to worry that
they've harmed the girl—these lads are bent, but not
known to be violent.'

John looked through the glass door at the two men who

were seated on wooden chairs at a table. Both were smoking, both looked defiant and the constable with them looked as if he as finding it hard to control his temper.

John was disappointed. 'They're too young and the wrong build,' he said, shaking his head. 'They're nothing like the man who wears leathers.'

Jamieson nodded. 'Early twenties, both around five-nine, employed as glaziers, would you believe. What better occupation for spotting what people have that's worth nicking and noticing who's away from home—plus they had your lists as a nice little extra. They'll end up pleading guilty and we'll get a fair bit of the stuff back.'

'They still had the lists?'

'A bit tattered but they still had them.'

That meant that the threats had nothing to do with Bridie running off and taking the photocopies with her, and these two didn't fit the biker's description at all.

'Do me a favour, mention a Mrs Pearson and see how they react.'

Jamieson pushed open the door and left John outside in the corridor. He couldn't hear what Jamieson said but he did see their reactions and didn't need Jamieson's negative report.

'I think we got the truth that time,' the policeman said. 'Anything else?'

'I thought all along that the biker was one of them and that he was Bridie's boyfriend,' John muttered. 'How about mentioning him and seeing how they react?'

Jamieson nodded. 'Will do.'

The two young men braced themselves with an attempt at off-hand bravado when they saw Jamieson come into the room again but their expressions soon changed. John could see the startled looks they exchanged and then there was a heated discussion and much shaking of heads. Jamieson was leaning on the table, resting on his spread hands with his grim face thrust close to the two young men and suddenly they looked scared—John knew that in their position Jamieson would have scared him too. At last the policeman

ended with a waving of a wagging finger and he left two
very subdued prisoners behind him when he rejoined John.

They moved further along the corridor and Jamieson was
grinning. 'That will get them talking. They want to make
a statement.'

'Do they know who the biker is?'

'They swear they never met Bridie and—' Jamieson
pulled the lobe of his ear—'I'm inclined to believe them,
but they're sticking to the story of getting the lists in a pub.'
He moved a couple of steps away and then swung back.
'They also say that a man in a leather jacket offered the
lists to them. They don't know if he owns a motorbike but
one reckoned he had a V-shaped logo on the front of the
sweatshirt he was wearing *underneath* the jacket—he didn't
pay any attention to the wording.'

'Do you believe them?'

Jamieson shrugged. 'I think so. I can't see any reason for
them to lie now and I can usually tell when we make a
breakthrough. It could be that they were trying to sell some
of the goods in a pub and the biker spotted them. I can't
understand why he would just hand the lists over to them,
though.'

'Neither can I.'

'Let's go and have a coffee in my room. It's not very
good, but at least it's better than your friend Tollis makes.'

They passed other officers in the corridor who stood aside
to let them by and Jamieson was treated with respect,
although he didn't seem to notice. He began to talk as soon
as the door of his office closed behind them.

'Bridie McGuire was persuaded to steal copies of your
empty properties by the man on the bike? Do you agree?'
He poured coffee from a jug and handed a cup to John.
'Why then hand those lists over to two thugs like that? For
what purpose?'

'Because he only wanted to look at them and then had
no further use for them.'

'Right.' Jamieson was like a hound on the trail of a fox.

'And he threatens you when you ask questions about the girl.'

'Or when he discovered I was looking for Mrs Pearson, *or* because . . . no, that can't be . . .'

'What can't?'

'I was looking for Mrs Pearson on behalf of Maria, who was then run down by a car.'

'Exactly.'

'Then are they all connected? Bridie, Maria and Mrs Pearson?'

Jamieson sat down heavily. 'I haven't a clue, but we'll find out. Tell me everything you've been doing.'

It took a long time. Jamieson recorded what he said to save him taking notes and in going over it all made it fresh again in John's mind. Jamieson seemed satisfied at the end of it.

'OK then. Now we'll both catch our breaths and think it over. It's quite a tangle, but then you usually do get caught up in interesting things. Dangerous too, unfortunately.'

'You'll let me know if anything develops?' John said.

Jamieson promised he would do that.

'And there's something more I should tell you,' John said, hesitating because he knew he was going to make Jamieson angry. Sitting in Jamieson's office, a modern extension which had a lot of windows draped with blinds, with charts and filing cabinets lining a wall and a desk that was not as substantial as the ones in Kramer House, made this an official discussion. It wasn't anything like the informal chats they often had. Functional was the best word to describe the room, and noisy.

The policeman had folded his arms.

'What would that be, I wonder—another excuse to have me working overtime?' He was in good humour, as if the tangled web had set his mind a puzzle that he would enjoy, so John took the plunge and told him about his car which was now parked around the back of the building.

'On the night when someone tampered with Maria's luggage, I think he got at my car at the same time.'

'What does "got at" mean, Mr Leith?'

John explained the details and waited for Jamieson to comment.

'And how many sets of fingerprints will there be now that you've removed the evidence?' The humour was fast disappearing.

'Garek's man touched only the length of brake pipe.'

Jamieson sighed. 'Then: 'Leave it with me,' he said. 'Don't let anyone else near the car and I'll get someone to look it over but don't hold your breath waiting for a good result. And I'd appreciate it if you kept me informed at the time that the many incidents in your life take place, not a day or two after or when you find the time to mention them.'

It was a valid censure and John felt properly chastised as he left the building, but he also felt certain that they were closing in on the man who had threatened him. Was Bridie in real danger from the man? He wanted to see her back with her mother. He wasn't sure about would happen when she did turn up but he supposed it all depended on whether or not Jamieson asked him to press charges against her. Being an employer had wider responsibilities than he'd ever imagined.

CHAPTER 10

There was a nip in the air that evening as he set off to visit Maria, but the sky to the west was a glorious red, promising a settled spell of weather. He managed to find a parking place close to the entrance to the wards which were behind the casualty department and that allowed him to nip quickly inside. He no longer had to think twice about being watchful—it was automatic to put himself in the safest possible situation. A man who had tried to poison him with carbon monoxide could just as easily come at him from any shadowy position with violence on his mind. Inside, it was brightly lit, there were plenty of people about and the Irish sister had news for him.

'There has been some improvement. She's coming out of it but only briefly at the moment. And she can respond when we speak to her.'

John looked at the still figure in the bed who was now breathing for herself. Her head was still bandaged but the graze on the side of her face had formed a scab. She looked very vulnerable, very young, and to him she still looked very ill. But even as he watched, her eyes flickered open and closed again.

'She's on the mend,' the sister repeated, but she didn't sound completely happy with Maria's condition—or was it the usual caution that accompanied every bulletin?

'Will she make a complete recovery?'

The sister pursed her lips. 'There is a degree of paralysis on her left side, but that shouldn't affect her speech—unless she's left-handed. In any case, we're hoping it may not be permanent.'

Paralysed. A surge of anger swept through him like an electric shock. He remembered Maria's joyful phone call with all the signs that the girl was beginning to realize that a small inheritance meant having fun. She had been looking forward to her sightseeing trip and now it might be months before she was able to walk.

'I had hoped to speak to her when she came around,' he said, almost to himself. 'To see if she remembered what happened.'

'That may never be possible. Patients often have no recollection of accidents—why is it so important that she remembers the accident? Her other visitor has been asking the same thing.' Her soft Irish brogue made 'thing' sound like 'ting'.

John felt his pulse quicken. 'How often has her other visitor been here?'

The sister's eyebrows went up. 'Nearly every day, the

same as you, but as her cousin that is understandable and he's most concerned for the poor girl.'

'I think I know him, tall man, heavy build?'

'Sure that's right. Sounds like him.' A nurse was at her elbow waiting to speak and the sister began to edge away.

'He's a motorbike fanatic—I expect he was still in his leather gear?' He attempted a smile while offering a prayer that she would say yes.

'No, he wasn't,' the sister called back to him. 'He's always very smart, in a suit.' Then she was gone.

A man who dressed smartly was waiting for Maria to show signs of recovering. That could be perfectly all right —if he was her cousin, but what if he had another motive? And what would he do if she was able to speak? He must have had the same report that the sister had given him, that Maria was coming out of the coma—so would that make the man doubly anxious. Maybe he hoped for the chance to put a pillow over her face to shut her up forever . . . Not in this ward where she was watched around the clock by nurses, but as soon as she was moved to an open ward she might be in danger. That meant that time was getting short and he had to find the biker before Maria woke up.

He drove back to Kramer House, knowing he needed to talk to Tollis.

'The thing is, he really could be her cousin,' he said. 'We don't know if Maria has relatives here from Lucy Simpson's side of the family.'

Tollis, dressed in dark polo-necked sweater and dark trousers, looked thinner in the face. The edge of his jaw was no longer softened by the extra weight he often carried, a penalty from sitting for too long at a desk. He looked all the better for it, harder and meaner. As usual, his dark hair was clipped short all over but it was damp, as if he'd just freshened up.

'He could simply be someone she met since she arrived here and he's pretending to be a relation so that he can get in to see her—people do that, you know, and you have to keep an open mind . . . She's a pretty girl and she could have found herself a boyfriend, but on the other hand I'm inclined to agree with your first reaction. You have an uncanny knack for smelling trouble and I'd pay my men double if they could learn how you do that.' He leaned forward and his eyes were hard. 'If the car ran her down on purpose I'd say that means that Maria knows who he is *and* what he's been up to. I'd lay my odds on money being at stake. Lots of it.'

'And Maria has some, but how would he get it by killing her?'

Tollis was frowning. 'I didn't mean Maria's money exactly—I was thinking more of a scam that Maria could connect him with—but I see what you're getting at and it's an angle to think about.'

'A cousin would inherit,' John said. 'If there really is one hanging about.'

'A distant one, who felt a bit cheated when he was left out of the will? Someone close to the old girl maybe, who expected to get the lot. But how much did Maria get, for Christ's sake? Did you get the impression she inherited enough to cause all this?'

'Those old houses can sell for quite a bit. Have you got today's *Scotsman*? It has the property section.'

Tollis salvaged it from a heap on the floor and they pored over the pages, comparing other house prices in the same locality. 'You've seen it; how many rooms would you guess?'

'Five or six, and attics, but the old girl might not have spent much on it. It could have needed quite a bit spent on modernization.'

'Still, we're talking a minimum of eighty thousand and to some people that's a lot of cash. Enough to kill for?' Tollis was showing the same keen interest as Jamieson now.

'Depends on the degree of desperation, someone who is in debt, in danger of losing a business—although the sister said he dressed smartly,' John reminded him. 'A real cousin from the Scottish side of the family who made himself known to Maria perhaps, discovered she wasn't parting with any of the loot and decided to take it anyway. How do I go about finding what relations Lucy Simpson had?'

'Ask the neighbours or get a copy of the will to see if there were any smaller bequests,' Tollis suggested.

'From Smith?' John wanted to avoid that if he could.

Tollis noted his pained expression and grinned. 'Still prejudiced because he came over as supercilious? I know exactly how you feel, but in this job you have to smile at all kinds of people for the sake of the information you want.'

'If I remember right you called him a bastard at one point.'

'In the heat of the moment. You can by-pass him by getting a copy from wherever they record such things. Try Register House on Princes Street—you'll need a copy of the old girl's death certificate anyway to pinpoint the date she died. It would be quicker to ask Smith.'

'Oh hell, he's a nit-picker. He'd want to know all the reasons why, every detail.'

'And you'd have to crawl a bit.' That seemed to tickle Tollis.

John gave in. 'OK, I'll phone him if I have to. There's something else, someone I saw at the motorbike showroom, who looked familiar. He might have worked for Rees at one time but I can't place him or even be sure it's Kramer's I associate him with.'

'I wasn't familiar with all of Rees's men—ask Personnel. Some of the men used passes—with photographs. Did you see that small paragraph in today's paper that Jamieson has arrested those two men?'

'I hope Bridie sees it. I've wasted a lot of time getting side-tracked because she didn't come forward.'

'You're enjoying it. You're like a hound with your nose on the trail—I see exactly the same thing all the time. No matter how tired the men are, when they get a job like this they come to life. It's an extra sense of some kind that only some people are born with, and you've got it.' He stubbed out his cigarette. 'Or it's sheer bloodymindedness, I've never worked it out.'

'Does it include getting scared?'

'You bet it does. The man who says he's never felt his bowels get loose is a liar.' Tollis stood up. 'Let's go eat.'

As they made for the restaurant the subject was still on his mind.

'There's a man around who cold-bloodedly aimed a car at a nice young girl and he got under your car and stuck in a tube that could have killed you and a lot of other innocent people if you'd caused a crash. That's enough to scare anyone, me included.'

'I'll find him,' John said. 'But time's getting a bit short.'

They turned into Tollis's favourite Italian restaurant and Tollis grunted. 'That's why I think Mike should be around to keep an eye on your back or to help with legwork, but I can't trust him for the moment. He's inclined to hit the bottle still, so I've told him to dry out fast.'

'Isn't that a bit hard considering what he's been through, losing his son?'

'I don't know any other way of handling him. Work is my only answer as far a he's concerned, but if he's not interested . . . It might help him to feel wanted,' he said as they waited for the food to arrive. 'This has been good experience for you, handling two things at once—you'll have to get used to that.'

Tollis was still taking it for granted that he would work for Sentinel one day, but wasn't he already doing that? He'd only spent a few hours at his desk in the last week and even then his presence had not been necessary.

Tollis ate his way through three courses, explaining that he had a long cold night ahead of him. 'We're keeping watch on a warehouse. Organized pilfering and since we're short-handed we won't be having meal breaks, not even a visit to the loo.'

'You sit in the car all night?'

Tollis tasted the coffee and made a face. 'We tried that last night but there was too much coming and going. Are you going to Clare's?'

'She's at the cinema with some friends.'

'Then do me a favour, keep an ear out for the phones; you can sleep in the back room on my bunk.'

John told the doorman he was taking calls for Mr Tollis and then he went up to Tollis's back room which was cramped, had probably once been a store for files. The bunk was just a thin mattress on a folding spring, the kind that is kept in a cupboard for casual visitors. There was an angled lamp clipped to the shelf above and some books. A spare suit hung on a hook on the wall and several shirts and underwear were on a shelf, plastic wrapped, as if they'd just come from the laundry. Home from home was more like a cell. He looked at the book titles: *To Kill a Mockingbird*, short stories by O. Henry, a couple of science fiction paperbacks and a book on forensic medicine—something to suit every mood. He settled for O. Henry and lay on the bunk fully clothed.

The light was still on and the book was lying on his chest when he was wakened around 2.0 a.m. The doorman was in the outer office holding a large brown envelope in his hand.

'Sorry to disturb you, sir. This came for you.'

John rubbed sleep from his eyes. 'When?'

'Minutes ago—I brought it right up. A special messenger I think—I heard his bike.'

John took the envelope gingerly, looked at it. It had his name on the front in large capitals and it was quite flat or he would have been suspicious. 'Thanks,' he said and the man left.

John tore it open and drew out a single sheet of paper on which there were words and a rough cartoon drawing.

Next time for real, the words said in black ink. The crude drawing was of a man lying on his back with a large dagger sticking from his chest. Below that the message continued, was scrawled, as if the fist holding the pen had been shaking with anger. *You are dead.* The drawing was childish, but the full stop had made a hole in the page.

He sat looking at it for a long time, waiting for the message to frighten him but it didn't. In any other situation he would have tossed it aside with a laugh as the work of a crank, but the man who had delivered this was not stupid, just desperate. It was the work of someone who had given way to an impulse, had risked handing it over to the door-man face to face. Desperate people made mistakes. He slipped the page back into the envelope without any real hope that there would be fingerprints on it apart from his own. Then he went down the stairs in search of the door-man. He found him sitting in his room, drinking tea.

'Since they started locking the outside door I get decent meal breaks,' the man said.

'Did you get a good look at the man who brought the envelope?'

'Aye. He was right under the light, but not his face—he had the helmet thing down. Gave me a bit of a fright.'

'Did he say anything?'

'Not really. Just held that out and walked away but I think he was laughing. Then I heard the bike—noisy thing it was.'

The Harley. No one would miss the sound of that engine.

'Did I do wrong? Should I have made him bring it in? Only with security tightened up I can't just let any old person into the building.'

'No, you were right not to let him in,' John sighed. 'But I would like to know what he looked like.'

'He had his glove off, had it tucked up under his arm, and I saw his watch. Massive thing with V shapes at the sides. It caught my eye, although it wasn't gold.'

'That was very observant of you, thanks,' John said, and the man looked pleased.

It sounded like the sort of thing a member of HOG would wear, an authentic accessory for a Harley fanatic and per-haps might help the man at Alvin's to trace him. Every little helped.

'Were you on duty the night Chief Inspector Jamieson asked about who had been in the building?'

The man was immediately on the defensive. 'I told him

I knew the men who had come on. I've seen both of them often but I can't be expected to know everyone by name, can I? And I can't help it if Mr Tollis doesn't know who I mean.'

'We're only interested in one of them. As you know, he sneaked into my flat. Could he be the same man who delivered the envelope tonight?'

The doorman thought hard and then shook his head. 'I don't think so, but it's hard to compare the two because I didn't get a proper look at the messenger. I can't keep track of who can come in. They ought to have passes.'

It was something to bear in mind but the offices were not meant to be security-conscious. They were open to the public during the day and various other visitors. John went back up this uncomfortable bed but didn't sleep much for the rest of the night. The doorman said the intruder worked in the building, might not be the biker but he wasn't sure. And Jamieson had suggested that someone on the Kramer staff might have put the idea of taking the lists into Bridie McGuire's head. It was one thing to look outside for the biker and his partner, but quite another thing to have one of them working in the building.

At 6.0 a.m. Tollis came back. He took the sheet of paper from the envelope and examined it, then made a face.

'Not very bright, is he? But the message is there even if it is over-dramatic.' He looked cold and tired.

'Any luck with the pilferers?'

'They had a night off. I'm going to snatch a bit of shut-eye.' John left him to it. He had a full day ahead of him.

He was at Register House as soon as it opened and getting a copy of Lucy Simpson's death certificate caused no problems. From it he discovered that she'd never married, and that she'd died on July 10 the previous year.

'You should find a copy of her will at the commissary office at the Sheriff's Court,' the man told him. 'It doesn't come here for some years.'

'Is it possible to trace this lady's other relations?'

'Well,' the man said, 'you could make a start from her birth certificate, but Simpson is a very common name so it could take a long time.' He seemed to have time to spare so he showed John how to go about it. A computer held the information and by going back to the time of Lucy's birth, the screen revealed that she'd been born in Aberdour in Fife. There was also a very long list of all the other Simpsons born at the same time in the whole of Scotland.

'You're lucky she was born in a small place,' he commented as he showed John how to narrow down the procedure by sticking to those born in the same village as Lucy. 'Then you have to look at the years before and after her birth to track down her siblings—if there are any. Anyway, that's the general idea, but it could take you all day,' he said as he went to attend to another customer.

It was time that he couldn't spare at the moment, John thought, as he walked back to the High Street via North Bridge. It was a lovely day, calm and fresh with just enough nip in the air to show that winter was on the way out. There were already a lot of shoppers about and he didn't feel at all exposed on the wide street. The cartoon had shown a man killed by a dagger which he assumed was symbolic, unless the biker was skilled with throwing-knives. In a way, the message with the drawing had been so crude that it had taken the edge off the threat and it had been the man's silence that had been more threatening. John had the feeling that his opponent was now being forced out into the open and that was exactly what he wanted—to see his face.

The Sheriff's Court was opposite Parliament Square but he was directed around the corner to the commissary office.

'I'd like a copy of a will but the only information I have is the date of the lady's death,' he told the man behind the counter.

He paid a £5 search fee, produced the death certificate and resigned himself to wait, but it didn't take long. The man came back and shook his head.

'There is no will registered for that person,' he said.

'But there must be. The estate has been settled.'

'Are you sure there was a will?'

John let out his breath in a long sigh. 'I'm pretty certain there was.'

The man looked as if he was well used to such situations. 'There may well have been and we just don't have it—there is no automatic registering of wills and we only get a copy if the solicitor, or the executor, applies to the Sheriff for confirmation after all the effects have been gathered in. And it can take a long time, a year or more, for the estate to be wound up. So you see it is not unusual that we don't have a copy.'

'I see. Thanks.' Back to square one and in this case that meant a phone call to Smith after all. As he walked back to Kramer House he tried to think of some other way to trace Maria's possible relations but had to admit in the end that Smith was his first step. He made the call from his office and Smith's secretary only put up a token resistance before putting him through, but from her tone gave the impression that Smith had either asked not to be disturbed, or that calls from Kramer House were unwelcome. And that was proved by Smith's forced cheerfulness. John heard it clearly as he spoke. 'What can I do for you, Mr Leith?'

'Sorry if I'm disturbing you but I'm trying to trace any other relatives of Maria Twarog—a Scottish connection. Did the old lady have any surviving relations apart from Maria?'

Smith answered with a hint of caution in his voice. 'Not as far as I know.' He sounded as if he was afraid to let any useful information slip between his lips and John wondered how to prise it out of him.

'So there were no other bequests in the will?'

There was no reply right away and the silence went on and on. At last Smith cleared his throat. 'Are you asking for details of the will?'

'Yes,' John said bluntly. 'I was hoping that if there were other bequests they would lead me to Maria's distant relations.'

'Ah. Well, there was only the one for Mrs Pearson.'

'So there was a will. A legal will?'

Smith's composure deserted him. 'Miss Twarog's affairs are no concern of yours. If she is seriously ill and the hospital needs information about relatives they can apply to me personally and not through an intermediary.'

'As far as I know the hospital isn't interested. This is part of a Sentinel investigation. You are quite certain that Maria has no cousins, for example.'

Smith made a tutting sound and John knew the man was rattled. He was sitting in his plush office, no doubt getting red in the face and that pleased John very much indeed.

'She may have twenty but as far as I know they are in Poland!'

John was determined to have the last word. 'Then perhaps you'll let the hospital know that the one who is visiting her most days is an impostor. You *are* supposed to be looking after her welfare, and who knows what he's up to.'

Smith sounded as if he was choking as John hung up the phone.

He'd gone too far, been extremely rude to an influential man, but he had no regrets at all. And it would have been worse if he'd asked why Smith had not yet got around to getting the will registered. No doubt the big man considered the Simpson estate too small to rate a lot of his attention and was in no hurry. Successful he might be, but efficient he was not.

He cleared the small amount of paperwork that Val had left out for him, tried to bring a smile to Val's face and failed, and was about to ask her about personnel records when his phone rang.

'Get my message, Leith?' The caller had his mouth close to the phone and it was as if he was breathing in John's ear.

John didn't need to ask who was calling but he stalled while he reached for the microphone of his small hand-held recorder. The microphone clicked against the phone as he inserted it between his ear and the receiver and then he had to juggle with the 'on' switch.

'Message? Yes, I got a message. You must enjoy creeping

around in the small hours. Why don't you come out in the open, show your face?' The red light glowed and the small tape revolved showing it was recording.

'Fuck you, Leith. You've been warned and you're asking for it.'

'I've heard that before.' He wanted to keep the man talking and kept his tone even, unruffled, in the hope that the man's anger would make him give something away.

'I'll spell it out, you stupid bastard. Stop meddling. We know you're watching the girl and it's none of your business. You don't know what you're getting into.' The man's voice was getting louder but he was still cautious.

'Threats won't work. If you try to harm me or Maria you'll only find others coming after you. I'm getting closer to you all the time and the police are getting copies of everything that I find out about you. Why don't you give up your stupid games?'

'Games? I'll show you what games are if you don't leave well alone. And it's too late for you. Too late, I'm telling you. You get out of my hair or I'll kill you, and her.' He had lost control and he seemed to realize it because then his voice dropped. When he spoke again it was with a menacing coldness. 'I'll kill you.'

The little tape captured it all. And when John replayed it later the last threat was still as chilling. The man meant every word.

CHAPTER 11

He played the tape for Tollis and the big man's only comment was that the caller sounded unhinged. He tapped the cassette with a finger.

'Let Jamieson hear it.'

'I'm seeing him this evening, but it's not much to go on.'

'It might be enough for him to put a man at the hospital to keep an eye on Maria, or to give the nursing staff an official warning to watch out for the girl's supposed "cousin".'

'I'm going to stay away from the hospital for a bit anyway, and that might keep our biker quiet. You know, this whole thing has been a muddle from the beginning.'

'Don't feel too badly about it. I made the same assumptions as you did,' Tollis said. 'You should go ahead with your break over the weekend, give yourself some time to think things through.'

'No. Clare's jumpy about anything to do with Sentinel and who can blame her? I haven't told her yet that the weekend is off and that's not going to make her feel any better.'

There was one more thing he wanted to do before Jamieson arrived and after he left the Sentinel office he drove back to the area and where Maria's great-aunt had lived. The old lady's housekeeper had been a great knitter, according to her church minister, and people with serious hobbies often stuck to one supplier, and in this case it would be a wool shop.

It was a long shot, but if Mrs Pearson had not moved too far away it was reasonable to suppose that she would still use her favourite shop. It was important that he find the woman since the man who rode the Harley Davidson had been so determined that he should not.

The main thoroughfare of the neighbourhood was Ferry Road. It had a bus route that served a large chunk of the city and it had many side roads leading off it to small pockets of shopping areas. John worked his way along it, crossing it and recrossing it to look for wool shops. He found two, but neither had Mrs Pearson as a regular customer. The owner of the second one pointed him in the direction of another, which had a small window that was packed with hand-knitted baby clothes and inside the shelves were covered with skeins of wool in rainbow colours. Plastic packets of it were heaped haphazardly around the floor and on the counters.

'Mrs Pearson has been a customer for years,' the assistant told him. 'She knits most of our window displays.'

John felt like hugging her. 'Has she been in recently?'

'Oh . . . a couple of weeks ago, I think. She bought . . . let me see . . . lemon yellow, for a new grandchild due this summer.'

Two weeks. 'Did she buy a lot—I mean, if she knits that much might she be running out soon?'

'She was taking it on holiday with her,' the woman said. 'But yes, she will certainly be back for more as soon as the holiday is over.'

'She didn't say how long she was going to be away?'

He got a shake of her head as he'd expected. 'Do you have her address?'

'We reserve wool for our customers but we only put their names on the packet and don't bother about addresses usually—certainly not in Mrs Pearson's case.' She was trying to be helpful and was now deep in thought. 'She did mention something about her new house not being ready yet and she was staying with relations, but I don't think she said where . . . Can't be far away though.' She saw John's disappointment.

'Is it urgent?'

'I do need to speak to her,' he said.

'Well, it won't be long before she's back. Why don't you leave a message and I'll see she gets it? That's the best I can do.'

John wrote his name and phone number on a piece of paper that the woman slipped into the packet of wool that Mrs Pearson had reserved.

'And tell her she can leave a message if I'm not around —a note of how I can contact her,' John said. But as he drove away he wondered what questions he would ask Mrs Pearson when he found her. She was involved in some way with the biker and might know his identity—that was the most he could hope for.

He took a detour as he headed back to Kramer House and drove along the road where Mrs Pearson had worked for Lucy Simpson. The house was still empty and he made a mental note to find out when it had been sold.

The offices were almost empty when Jamieson arrived just after five. The staff could finish at four on Fridays and this was the interval before they were all gone and the cleaners arrived. He offered Jamieson a Scotch which the policeman sipped as John played him the recording of the phone call. 'Nasty,' Jamieson said. He leaned back in his chair, crossed his legs, and John glimpsed black socks and shoes with a high polish. The policeman's trousers had a knife-edge crease, and this at the end of his working day. Jamieson put the empty glass down on the low table at his elbow. 'Let's do a re-cap of all we know about this biker.'

So John went back to square one and the biker's first phone call, but Jamieson interrupted.

'That's an assumption for a start—that it's the man on the motorbike who makes contact with you,' he pointed out. 'We know there is more than one—maybe just the two men—involved, but we don't really know who the front man is.'

'You're right,' John admitted. 'That's because I thought at first there was only one man, but at least we know now that he's not Bridie's boyfriend and has nothing to do with the burglaries. He doesn't want me to talk to two, and possibly all three, women—hence the threats. I haven't a clue why that upsets him.'

'And its important enough for him to tamper with your car and now add this new threat against you and Maria,' Jamieson said thoughtfully. He waved his hand in a negative way when John offered to refill his glass with whisky. 'And that house is still empty.' He narrowed his eyes as an artist does when trying to get the perspective right. 'I'd like a look inside there but I'd never get a warrant.'

'You think there could be something inside, a clue?'

'Empty houses are good storage places but he'd have to know the plans of the new owners. I wonder why they're in no hurry to occupy the place? Could be it was bought by an agent and they're just not ready to move. They could be abroad, have any number of reasons for leaving the place empty. There's nothing to involve me officially at the moment, apart from finding your Harley owner, of course. If you get any clues to his identity I'll pull him in.'

'Maria and Mrs Pearson have never met, as far as I know, and that's the really puzzling thing,' John said.

'But they are connected by the will—both are mentioned in that,' Jamieson said quietly.

'And Ambrose Smith, the lawyer, is not exactly helpful, although he did say that there were no other beneficiaries and as far as he knows, no other relatives in this country.' He dropped his head into his cupped hands and then dragged his fingers tiredly down his face. 'I can't figure it out.'

'You will,' Jamieson said encouragingly. His eyes sparkled with something close to humour. 'Just get the smallest bit of evidence and I'll step in.'

John's head came up. 'Do you have your own ideas on what this is all about?'

Jamieson stood up but didn't answer the question directly. 'I've got a feeling about it. Enough to make the back of my neck tingle because it's beginning to resemble something I've handled before.' He held up a bent index finger that almost touched his thumb. 'This big at the moment but it grows every time we talk. I find it useful to bounce ideas around with you. We'll solve it,' he said, nodding as he made for the door. Then he paused and snapped his fingers. 'Let's get the bastards,' and he grinned his policeman's grin. He looked very like Tollis at that moment, when the big man was close to the end of an investigation, smelling the quarry, closing in for the kill.

John waited in the quiet room for a long time after he'd gone, going over the whole series of events which had started with his uncle's funeral and the legacy of the Kramer company that had dropped unwanted into his lap. Maria too had appeared on the scene because of a legacy, and then there had been the confusion of the false trail caused by Bridie McGuire. Yes, it was helpful to exchange thoughts with the policeman, but although the next moves were clearer, he still had no idea where the investigation was leading. Jamieson had a hunch that made the back of his neck tingle and he had the experience to sniff such things out.

'Wish I had,' John sighed. He got up and turned off the main light and then stood looking down on the dark street below. There was the usual amount of traffic for a Friday evening and several cars were parked on either side of the street and a watcher could be sitting in any one of them. He had to take the man's threat seriously if only for Clare's sake, so he reached for the phone.

'You got me out of the bath. I'm dripping on the carpet.'

'Change of plans. I'll meet you at the restaurant; I'll take a taxi.'

'I could just as easily pick you up,' she said.

'I'd rather you didn't.'

'Ah.' That meant she accepted his comment but would question him about it later.

'Just don't be late. I hate getting there first,' she said.

'And we'll have to call off the weekend,' he said. 'I'm sorry.'

'But I'm all packed. Damn it, John, you could have told me sooner.' Then she hung up before he could say any more.

Luck was on his side when he eventually left the building to meet her because as he flagged down a taxi, the lights changed to red, so that anyone thinking of following him would be held up, and as he walked the length of Rose Street, he was as sure as he could be that he had no one on his tail. Clare was already sitting at the table he'd reserved in the small back room of the restaurant owned by a Swiss couple. The lights were low, the tables shielded by the high backs of the seats, an illusion of privacy in what would probably be a crowded room before very long.

'All right, I was early,' Clare said. She was still angry but she never clung to a mood for long. She would either have it out or accept the inevitable and he just had to wait and see which she would choose. Her dress was black and had transparent sleeves to her wrists; her only jewellery was gold earrings and a gold chain around her neck. He liked the chain. There was something sexy about a delicate gold chain on a slender neck, especially when glossy dark hair was just touching it, swinging with her every movement.

'Happy birthday,' he said quietly as he passed the flat box across the table and watched as she draped the bracelet around her wrist.

'It's lovely.' The bracelet slid up on the black sleeve of her dress as she rested her elbows on the table, clasped her fingers under her chin. 'I like it.' She smiled her pleasure, but she was still having trouble with the anger.

'So tell me why we had to arrive separately. Was it because your assistant was coming here too? Is this part of a Sentinel mystery?' There was a brittleness in her voice that was quite unlike her.

'Val?' He began to look around but Clare stopped him.

'Don't. She hasn't seen you and I don't want to share the meal with them.'

'Them?'

'She's with a bad-tempered-looking man in the other room. I saw them sit at the table and now I can just see the man through the doorway—so you didn't know she was coming here?'

'What difference does it make if Val uses the same restaurant? But no, I didn't. She's not been in a talkative mood for some time and she never mentions her private life anyway.'

Clare looked at the menu and he got the feeling that the evening that had started badly was going to get worse. The waiter arrived and took their order.

'About the weekend,' John said. 'Something came up. We can go next week if you like.'

Clare moved her shoulders in an it-doesn't-matter gesture and then pushed her food around the plate.

'You didn't explain why you had to come by taxi,' she

said. She had ordered duck in a dark cherry sauce but she'd
hardly touched it and he knew that she was not going to
be satisfied with an evasive answer. But he couldn't tell her
the exact truth either.

'At the time it seemed the best thing,' he said, leaving it
to her to work it out, knowing she would not find that
difficult.

She nodded. 'Sentinel again. Why can't you find enough
to do in Kramer's?' She closed her eyes as if trying to control
her emotions and when she looked at him again he saw that
there were angry tears in them.

'It's my birthday. Do I have to share that with . . . The
evening is spoiled and I think I'd like to go home,' she said.
'I'm not in the mood for this.'

'At least have coffee and talk,' he suggested, but her eyes
were on something behind him and he guessed that Val and
her companion had finished their meal and were leaving.

'I don't think they enjoyed it either,' Clare said drily as
she reached for her bag. 'Val looks upset . . . there's something about men who wear camel coats . . .'

John whirled around to look, saw no one and got up and
moved through the tables in the other room. Outside, he
was just in time to see Val and her companion enter a taxi
at the end of the street and as it moved off he saw the side
view of the man's head. There was no doubt that it was the
same man who had avoided him in Alvin's showroom.

'Bloody hell,' he muttered as he went back inside to pay
the bill and collect an angry Clare. 'Sorry. I wanted to get
a better look at him.'

'So you did know they'd be here—it's just another part
of Sentinel business.'

They were in her car, with Clare in the driving seat but
she made no move to turn on the ignition. 'I tried not to
mind, I really did, when you got mixed up with Tollis
again.' She was staring straight ahead. 'But it's going to be
there all the time, isn't it? It's not like an office job where
you turn off the lights and go home—it's never finished.

You have to be on call twenty-four hours a day—no wonder Tollis has no private life.'

John sat and listened and knew he had no answer. It had been bothering her and it was better out in the open.

'I had no idea that Val would be there tonight,' he said at last. 'But I've been looking for that man and—'

'And it couldn't wait? You could ask Val in the office on Monday who he was—there was no need to go running off and leaving me standing there like an idiot.'

From her viewpoint that was true, but she didn't know about the urgency of finding the man so that young Maria would be safe. 'It's very important that I find out who he is.'

'Of course it is. Sentinel will always come first. I suppose this is why the weekend is off as well?'

'Yes, it is. I can't leave now.'

She was nodding, as if that was exactly what she'd expected. She turned to look at him and her eyes were full of pain. 'I was told today that I'm being transferred to London. I was going to talk it over with you, but—' she gave a tremulous sigh—'I don't think I need to now. It's probably the best thing that could happen—at least I won't know what you're getting involved in.' She switched on the engine. 'I suppose you'll want to confer with Tollis, so I'll drop you at Kramer's.'

John said nothing. He was too numb to take in what she was saying. As the car swung down towards Princes Street and up the Mound, all he could note was that it had begun to rain. The good spell of weather was over and he could only hope that it was all that was ending. The car pulled up outside the Kramer building and Clare kept the engine running.

'When are you leaving?' John asked.

'In three weeks but I'm going down for a visit first, to meet people, see about accommodation and things. I think I'll do that next week,' she said quietly. Her face was resolute, stiff.

'I'll see you before you go.' He took it for granted that they would talk but Clare shook her head.

'No . . . I don't know. Maybe I should do some thinking about all this. I'll call you when I know how I feel about it.'

'Don't leave it too long.'

She nodded but didn't look at him.

'Clare, we need to talk about this.'

'I know, but not now.'

He got out of the car and watched her drive away, then went into the building.

'You've always known her career comes first,' Tollis pointed out.

'No, it hasn't. It's the danger aspect that bothers her and I can't promise her that it won't ever happen again. So I can't blame her.'

He couldn't expect Tollis to understand the special sort of relationship he and Clare had and he didn't want to discuss it. Tollis seemed to know that and he asked questions instead.

'What's this about Val?'

'She was in the restaurant with the man in the camel coat. He was the man I saw at Alvin's and now I'm wondering if he is her husband.' John described him and Tollis nodded.

'Sounds like him, but that's not sinister. George Forbes might have avoided you in the motorbike place because he's been upsetting Val recently and he knows you're her boss.'

All John's instincts told him otherwise. 'Did he work for Rees?'

Tollis settled back for a long session, lit a cigarette, and rested his arms on his desk. 'As far as I know he still does, or did until very recently. He's a valuer, a surveyor, based in the other section in the Royal Mile.'

And John remembered Val's reluctance to visit that building; now he knew why.

Tollis went on: 'He drinks a lot and sometimes he messed

up his work because of it, arrived late and that sort of thing. Rees put up with the work complaints from customers for Val's sake for a while, but when clients lose a property because they couldn't get a surveyor on time . . . well, it got too much and Rees finally moved him to a less responsible job. It was all very difficult. As far as I know he and Val managed to avoid bumping into each other—you know how that side of the business seems to run itself—and it's only lately he's been in touch for some reason. She's not likely to bleat to you or me about him.'

'But she has been in contact with him lately.'

'She did mention it.' Tollis spoke evenly. 'We had a thing going some time back but, like Clare, Val has other priorities and to be honest it wasn't worth the hassle.'

John guessed that the tone hid a lot of other emotions.

'And now she's going out with him again?'

Tollis lifted his shoulders in a tired shrug. 'I doubt that unless there is a good reason—maybe to get the message across that she wants nothing to do with him.'

'I'll have to speak to her about it,' John said. 'If only to get it cleared up. Her husband did panic when he saw me that day.'

Tollis looked at him with an open expression. 'She won't hide anything but she's prickly about her private life.'

'I'll be tactful. Where does she live? I don't want to wait until Monday.'

Tollis wrote it down and slid the piece of paper across to him. 'It's what I would do as well,' he said. He smiled slightly. 'You're developing a thick skin.'

Not thick enough, John thought bleakly as he drove towards Val's home. Clare could pierce it without any trouble at all, but he pushed that out of his mind. Right now he had to decide what to do if Forbes had taken Val home and was still at her house.

He wasn't. Val was surprised to see him on her doorstep but she invited him into her sitting-room and there was no one else there. She switched the television off and he saw that she was still wearing a dark blue dress, probably the one she'd dined in, but had slipped off her shoes. After he was seated, she curled up in an easy chair, tucking her feet under her. She looked perfectly relaxed, as if there had been no quarrel with an ex-husband in the recent past.

'We were in the same restaurant tonight,' he said and she looked surprised. 'I was in the other room,' he explained and wondered if he imagined the slight wariness that appeared in her eyes.

'Is that why you're here? I don't understand.'

'This isn't easy, Val. I'm not prying but I need to know about the man you were with.'

She slid her legs to the floor as her body stiffened. 'I was with George Forbes, my ex-husband, but that's really none of your business,' she said. Now she was frowning but he saw that at the same time she was curious.

'You know that I do some work for Sentinel? Well, your husband may be part of an on-going investigation but I'm not sure. I just want to eliminate him. Is there any reason why he should panic at the sight of me? Why he should run off when we met casually?'

'Not that I know of. George is a strange mixture, weak in some respects but persistent in others. I don't think I ever got to know him well. What sort of thing could he be involved in?'

'Would he threaten violence?'

She drew in her breath and held it for a long time. 'I'm sure he wouldn't, but when we were married . . . he might hit a woman, but if he was facing another man . . . he's a coward, I think.'

'Does he own a motorbike?'

This time there was no hesitation. 'No. He likes comfort too much, I can't see him riding that sort of machine in all weathers.'

'What sort of car does he drive?'

'I don't know. I don't see him at all but tonight he used a taxi.'

The next question was difficult to ask but he had to do

it. 'Is he the sort of man who would use a woman to get something he wanted?'

She gave a straight answer. 'George Forbes would use anybody to get what he wants.'

John nodded to show he appreciated her honesty. 'And has he asked any questions recently about Kramer's, or about me in particular?'

She was angry. 'I never discuss . . .' She stopped, blinked. 'He asked about my job—the chance of my getting on the board, but I thought he was trying to find out my financial situation.' She stopped, then seemed to decide that she had to go on. 'This is not something I like to talk about. My husband pays nothing in maintenance and I thought he was afraid I would make demands now that my son is getting older. When he talked about the future of Kramer's, whether you would work for Sentinel, I thought it was part of the same thing.'

'So he did ask if I worked for Sentinel?'

'Yes,' she said slowly. 'He made a joke of it, said what sort of things could you do for them. I didn't know and I said so.'

'He wouldn't like that.'

'No, he didn't. Is that why he got in touch with me, to find out about you? Why would he want to know what you were doing for Sentinel?'

'I'm beginning to work that out,' John said drily. 'But I'll find out for sure. Where is he working now?'

'I only found out tonight that he has left Kramer's. I expect he's in the same sort of work—I didn't ask.'

John got up and Val followed to the door. She was quite small without her high heels, a different person in her own home.

'I'm sorry,' she said and the words had a wealth of meaning. She was sorry her private affairs were getting mixed up in business, sorry she'd spoken to George Forbes about him. 'I only met him tonight because he was being persistent. He wouldn't listen when I told him on the phone that as far as I'm concerned, he no longer exists. I think I finally got through to him. But now it seems he was still using me, to find out about you.'

'It's all right,' John assured her. And he was certain that was true, but he was just as sure that her husband was up to no good, because Forbes was one man who could slip into Kramer House without raising the suspicions of the doorman. He could have searched the flat while his accomplice put a piece of red brake pipe under John's car.

CHAPTER 12

It was after eleven when he left Val's and the streets were quiet. He mulled over what they had discussed and he knew that he was getting close to the biker. Finding Forbes shouldn't be too difficult, even if Edinburgh was full of surveyors, and Forbes would lead him to the biker because the one must know the other.

He drove automatically, his mind busy on a possible connection between the two men. He was certain now that the man who owned the Harley was the one who has issued the threats in person or on the phone because Val had agreed that her husband was not the type.

Forbes, the weaker man, was more likely to crack if questioned but until there was some definite evidence against him, Jamieson's hands were tied. John spun the wheel and turned into the side of the building and parked in his usual place, but then paused with his hand on the door handle.

The parking area at the back of the Kramer building was in darkness and that made him instantly alert. The security light on the wall was off and it shouldn't be. He knew that it was the incoming doorman's duty to check it each night and the last shift had started at ten. There could be a valid reason why the light was off, a bulb blown since it was checked, but he sat in the car for some time all the same. He could see nothing out of the ordinary. All the cars were Kramer cars, no one was lurking in the shadows, but to be on the safe side he took a heavy torch from the glove compartment and gripped it tightly as he got out of the car.

He fell over the doorman's body almost immediately, hidden as it was in the shadow of the car next to his. He bent to run his hands over the man's belt where his keys usually hung but they were missing—that could only mean that an intruder was now inside the building and if he had the doorman's bunch of keys he would have access to every room. Tollis could be dozing on his bunk, unaware of the danger.

The doorman's body was warm and blood still oozed from a head wound, his breathing was quiet and regular. John left him where he was and moved around the side of the building. He looked up and down the street, hoping for a cruising police car, but there was none and he couldn't waste time looking for a phone-box that might be vandalized anyway. He was on his own.

The front entrance was brightly lit as he slotted his own key in the lock. There was a phone in the room where the men took their tea-breaks and that was where he headed first. There was no sound, no radio playing in the Sentinel rooms above, where men often stayed late to write up reports or to exchange information. That was to be expected since they were all working overtime and the building had been empty quite often in the past week. Where would the intruder go?

He cursed the elegant marble tiles of the hall when gravel on his shoes made it impossible to move quietly but he reached the room at the side of the hall without incident. There he found that the phone had been pulled from the wall. Every nerve in his body tingled with the urge to leave and seek help before he went any further, but the possibility that Tollis was in danger made him head for the stairs.

The Sentinel Agency had a half-glazed door revealing that all the inner rooms were in darkness and he hesitated, unsure whether to go in or to check his own floor on the upper level. The deciding factor was that the nearest telephone was in the Sentinel office and there was also the possibility that Tollis was asleep in the back room. But would the biker—if that was who the intruder was—expect him to do just that? Was he inside the office, patiently waiting? Would his anger be building up, ready to explode as soon as John opened the door? He realized he was breathing very shallowly and that sweat was forming in a slick covering all over his body.

Then a group of youths out in the street made a sudden commotion as they passed the door and as they lingered, scuffling and shouting among themselves, John flattened himself against the wall and waited, knowing that their voices would cover any sound from inside the dark office. His heart was hammering.

They moved on at last and their voices gradually faded. An occasional car going up the road was the only sound apart from his breathing. He began to move, walking on carpet as he edged forward to open the Sentinel office door, let it drift wide. He paused, knowing with some sixth sense that the man was in there waiting for him. He could feel the other presence as surely as if he was brushing against him, but where was he?

There was very little light because this main office was an internal room without windows, but some was coming faintly from the floor below. It barely penetrated the room but it was enough to define the shape of his body as he moved cautiously forward. The intruder would certainly see him and might already be moving towards him. John slipped inside, closed the door behind him, and quickly moved forward, keeping his body low.

He knew the exact position of every desk and chair. There was a straight passage leading to Tollis's office and his sleeping quarters beyond that, but it was never a tidy room and he was as likely to fall over a waste basket or someone's forgotten sports bag.

'I know you're here,' he said and the sound of his own voice in that large room rang out loud and challenging. He moved quickly and ducked down behind a desk, waiting for some movement and when it came he bent further until he was almost lying on the floor. The chair that came flying across the room hit the wall behind him and was too accurate for comfort. He reached up and let his hand seek a phone but he only managed to dislodge a file that fell with a slithering sound to the floor. There was a rush of footsteps as the intruder headed in his direction, desks were nudged out of the way, things fell to the floor, and the other man began to curse. John was on his feet and turning towards the sounds when the room was suddenly full of blinding fluorescent light.

John felt naked, pinned to the spot. Tollis stood in the doorway, a large dishevelled figure still half asleep.

'What the hell's going on here?' he roared, advancing.

'Get back,' John shouted, turning to face the biker across the room. The light had startled him too, and for an instant all three stood frozen, then the biker began to move in a direct line towards the door. The light gave highlights to the black helmet, illuminated the man's powerful body, bulky in the leather jacket, and he moved so fast that he took desks and chairs and stacks of files with him, like a ship surging through a heavy sea.

John moved at a tangent to cut him off and Tollis, fully awake now, took in the situation and hurled himself after John. More desks and chairs were toppled as he headed for the intruder, once he staggered and nearly fell, and all the time he was roaring with anger. There was no doubt that Tollis on the warpath made the man move faster—it certainly swept John forward without a thought of what would happen when he was face to face with the man in black. The three met at the glass door and the biker crashed into it, smashing the glass and rattling the wooden frame so hard that the building seemed to shudder. In the moment that John was knocked back against Tollis, the biker was out in the hallway, then he whirled and crouched.

John and Tollis both skidded to a halt when they saw the knife he was holding. The blade was ten inches long and it glinted, the tip tapered to a wicked point but Tollis reached behind him and came up with a moulded plastic chair, the chrome legs a defence against the blade. The man hesitated now that he had two adversaries who both matched him in height, and one of whom was equally broad.

'Just try it, you bastard,' Tollis muttered and the knife point wavered, swung slightly in John's direction, then back again, and not being able to see the man's face made him all the more terrifying. The visor blacked out everything, the intention that must be in his hidden eyes, the fear that he too must be feeling, or the anger that his plan had gone very wrong.

It was a frozen tableau that lasted for moments but seemed like an age, then the intruder began to back away, still bent towards them, and John saw that his jacket gleamed with small particles of broken glass. Tollis followed, jabbing with the chair like a lion tamer.

'Stay back,' he said as John began to follow him and they both watched the man go backwards down the stairs, steadying himself with one hand on the banister rail. When he was ten feet away, Tollis backed into the office and picked up a phone and John moved forward to stand at the top of the stairs.

The biker paused. His voice came upwards in a deep growl. 'Come on, Leith. Try to stop me.' The knife jerked upwards as if the man could imagine pushing it into John's abdomen and he gave a sort of frustrated moan. 'Come on, you interfering bastard.' And as if he couldn't bear to lose this last chance he came at a rush back up several steps, but Tollis emerged from the office and stood shoulder to shoulder with John.

'The police are coming,' he said coldly. Then he reached for the torch that John was surprised to find he was still clutching, and he hurled it at the man's head. It broke the tension as it caught the man a glancing blow and in a tumbling run he was down the stairs and out of the door.

'Come on,' Tollis said, taking the stairs three at a time, but they heard the sound of a car before they stepped on to the pavement. It took the corner at speed and was gone.

'He had a friend waiting for him, but it was worth a try and I only got part of the number,' Tollis growled as John followed him back into the building.

'We'll need an ambulance—he clobbered the doorman and took his keys,' he said, and he sat down in the nearest chair while Tollis phoned again.

'Why the hell did you come here anyway?' Tollis said angrily. He fetched a blanket and headed for the door.

'In case he cut your throat while you slept,' John said wearily.

'I might have been out.'

'I couldn't take the chance. I could smell that damned coffee machine as soon as I opened the door.'

They covered the unconscious doorman with the blanket from Tollis's bunk and heard the distant sound of a siren. Rain fell gently on them as they waited, the soft rain of a mild spring night, and Tollis looked up at the stairs as if saying a prayer.

'Thanks,' he said. 'It was stupid but it took guts. In future put your own safety first unless you are working with a partner.'

'I thought that was what I was doing,' John told him and Tollis grunted.

The police car was followed by the ambulance but the doorman was already waking up. They took him to hospital anyway and the two policemen followed John and Tollis into the building. Tollis did the talking and kept the statement simple. A man had knocked out the doorman and then used the keys to get in. Nothing was missing but probably the intention was to take anything portable or the like. The police were used to such things and went away with a parting comment that a security firm should be more secure, shouldn't it? That made Tollis fume.

'But they are so right. I'll have video cameras in tomorrow—no need in the past because who in their right mind would try to break in here, and for what?'

He was putting the office furniture back to some form of order, angrily banging piles of files on to desks, then stood angrily looking at the broken glass from the door. In his own office his coffee had simmered down to a concentrated liquid but it seemed to be just how he liked it. 'I've got a night shift,' he said. 'But I'll get another man in to mind the door before I leave.' They both had a Scotch while they waited for the man to arrive and after Tollis left, John went up to the flat and fell into bed. He was asleep in seconds.

He woke early and remembered what had happened the night before. Then he thought about Clare and knew that there was nothing stopping him withdrawing from the whole affair. She was right. It was stupid to take risks, to end up facing a man with a knife, but at the same time he knew that he had to see it through to the end.

No one worked in Kramer's on Saturdays and that meant he couldn't question his own surveyors about where Forbes might be working. He lay in bed and tried to work out what Forbes and the biker could be up to that made them so desperately afraid he would put the finger on them. Mentally he ticked off the connections between Mrs Pearson, Maria, and the two men and the answer was staring him in the face. Valuation of property was the work Forbes was in; Maria and Mrs Pearson were connected to a house that was still vacant months after it had been sold . . . to whom? He jumped out of bed, showered and was out of the building in half an hour, heading for the ESPC, the biggest property market showroom in Edinburgh. It took some time, but in the end he discovered that Lucy Simpson's house had not been advertised for sale there.

'It's easy enough to find out who bought it, though,' a helpful assistant told him. 'Meadowbank House is where all sales are registered, but it isn't open today.'

Back at the flat his hand hovered over the phone. He wanted to speak to Clare. He couldn't blame her for focusing her anger on Sentinel, his job, the way their future was shaping up, but it didn't mean they had to split up, for Christ's sake. In the end he decided to give her the time she needed to think things over.

He phoned the hospital instead. A nurse answered. 'Miss Twarog is making progress.'

'I know it's not visiting hours, but could I come and speak to her?'

The nurse wasn't sure and said she would have to check first and the next voice on the phone had the unmistakable accent of the Irish sister.

'Is that Mr Leith? We've been warned to screen Maria's visitors but you're welcome—she's been asking after you but don't expect too much. She's out of danger, but not herself yet.'

John took a car from the pool and drove straight to the Western, relieved that someone had issued instructions for Maria's safety. She was still pale, but there was glad recognition in her eyes when she saw him. She tried to smile but it dragged at the corner of her mouth. He was appalled that a pretty girl should be disfigured in such a way, but knew he had to be cheerful.

'Awake at last.'

'I don't remember much about it,' she said with difficulty. 'But the nurses told me you've been here.'

'I've got your luggage. Is there anything you need?'

She shook her bandaged head slightly and at that moment the sister came in with Maria's shoulder-bag. 'Here you are. It came with you in the ambulance.' She turned to John with a smile. 'Her lipstick, would you believe? She's had me turning out the property cupboard so that I could fetch her lipstick for you coming.'

John watched as the sister opened and brought out the lipstick and then applied it carefully to the drooping mouth. He saw Maria's left hand lying lifeless on top of the sheet and anger simmered, along with a vow to make the men who had done this pay a heavy price.

'There,' the sister said, admiring the transformation. Pale pink lipstick, a flick of blusher to pale cheeks, made all the difference and Maria's eyes sparkled. The girl had guts.

'And I'll put your watch and your change purse here—

she's after sweets from the trolley when it comes around,'
she added. 'She'll be up and running in no time.'

Would she? He doubted that.

Maria looked as if the small effort had tired her. The bag
gaped open on the bed and John could clearly see an envelope with the name of Ambrose Smith on its reverse.

'Did the solicitor send that to you after the estate was
settled?' he asked.

Maria touched the envelope and frowned, as if she
couldn't remember what it was. 'Oh yes. I brought it with
me in case I had to prove who I was.' She giggled, softly and
breathlessly. 'Now I can hardly remember why I needed to
do that.'

'You wanted to collect your painting,' he said quietly,
thinking that it seemed an age since she first come into the
Sentinel office with such an innocent request. 'Does it give
details of your aunt's will, Maria?'

'Yes. And what everything was sold for.' She was close
to exhaustion. 'Read it for yourself,' she said. The pink
lipstick made her skin seem paler than ever and he knew
he shouldn't stay much longer. He reached into the bag
and withdrew the letter.

It was well set out, on good quality paper, the items that
added up to her inheritance. John let his eyes go down the
column until he reached the final total, and that made him
gasp. He went back to the beginning and this time looked
at each entry carefully. The last deduction was for Ambrose
Smith's expenses and they were remarkably modest. By the
time he had refolded the letter Maria was nearly asleep
again.

'Would you mind if I borrowed this?' he said.

She smiled and closed her eyes and John slid the envelope
into his pocket. Before he left the hospital he paid a visit to
the shop run by volunteers and bought Maria some sweets
and magazines and a bottle of fruit squash. As another
thought occurred to him he added some talc and scented
soap to his purchases. Back in the ward he saw that she

was still sleeping, but at least her locker was no longer bare and looked more like the others.

He drove back in the Saturday morning traffic with a light drizzle misting the windscreen, knowing he needed advice of the sort that was probably out of Tollis's experience. Then he remembered what Gumley had said about Garek, that the man had once been a practising lawyer.

Glaziers had arrived to repair the door to the Sentinel office as he passed on his way up to the flat to call Garek, but before he could reach the phone, it rang.

'Mr Leith?'

It was Mrs McGuire's voice and his first reaction was guilt because he hadn't had the time to check and see how she was. Then he sensed that she was also being very tentative.

'Have you heard from Bridie?' he prompted her.

'Yes . . . Could you come to see me?'

'Well . . .'

'Today? I really wish you would,' she said.

John agreed, although he would rather have gone to see Garek first.

'I'll be there as soon as I can.'

There was no mistaking her relief as she hung up.

Then he dialled Gumley's home and, as usual, Garek answered. 'I have been trying to reach you, Mr Leith. The list of possible owners of that sportster model is getting shorter.'

'I was going to ask if I could come to see you anyway,' John said. 'I need some advice.'

They arranged that John would get there after lunch and Garek had one more question. 'Does David come back today?'

'Tomorrow, but the boys don't usually get free time after a trip. It's a tiring journey.'

'Pity. Mr Gumley would have enjoyed a visit from him.'

Before he left to see Mrs McGuire, he went to see if Tollis had had any more thoughts on the intruder, but Tollis was in a foul mood and he hadn't even bothered to shave. The men who were in were keeping out of his way and John heard one mutter that another load of stuff had disappeared from the industrial estate they were watching during the night. 'We can't cover the whole complex, so what does he expect?'

That gave the clue to Tollis's bad temper. 'I need to take on more men but that gets expensive when work is slack. I can spare someone to work with you, though. I don't want you poking around on your own.'

'Not necessary today but I could do with an extra pair of legs on Monday. Today I'm going to have Garek for company.' He almost reached for the envelope in his pocket as Tollis's eyebrows went up, but the big man was in the sort of mood where he didn't really want to listen. His attention was on the men who were hovering in the next room.

'I'll see you later, then,' Tollis said. 'Right now I've got to find out what the hell went wrong on that site last night. Watch yourself,' he warned at the last moment.

The glaziers were clearing up the debris of broken glass as John left and he wondered if by any chance some of it had worked its way down inside the biker's clothing. He hoped so.

Mrs McGuire was almost sheepish as she asked him into the flat and he soon saw why. A girl he took to be Bridie was sitting on the lumpy sofa, drying her long hair with a towel. She looked scared, dropped the towel on to her lap and he saw the mark of an old bruise on the side of her face.

'She came home yesterday and told me what she'd done.' The mother seemed both pleased to have her back, and ashamed that her daughter had caused her employer a lot of trouble. Bridie just clutched the towel and said nothing. Some people, John thought, were better-looking than their photographs, but that didn't apply to Bridie McGuire. The thought should have roused fresh sympathy for her but all he could feel was a dull anger. He wanted to reach out and shake her.

'Will she lose her job?' the woman asked, and behind the words John guessed there was financial worry. The girl's income paid for the extras that made life bearable.

He sat down. 'Tell me about it—how it all started.'

She looked nervously at her mother.

'I didn't think it was wrong—what Mr Forbes asked me to do.'

'Forbes asked you . . . ?'

She nodded, wide-eyed. 'He said he needed a note of all the empty properties that were on the computer. I often had to print out part of the list, for reports and things.'

'And what happened then?'

She looked at her mother again and flushed. 'When he came for them he said I'd done a good job and would I like to go out for a meal. I said yes.'

Val had said that the girl was looking for a man and it seemed she had been right. Bridie hadn't needed to be asked twice and Forbes would be quite a catch for her.

She stopped and her hands twisted the towel in her lap. Her mother was hanging on every word and John was sure it was making Bridie more nervous.

'Could you make some coffee, Mrs McGuire?'

She went reluctantly but Bridie looked relieved.

'Did you know why he wanted the lists?' he asked the girl.

'No. I did print-outs often for other people.'

'And after he took you out . . . ?'

She flushed. 'I went to his flat.'

'And he took you out again?' Another nod.

'Why did you phone me?'

She took a long, trembling breath. 'George said I couldn't go back to work again because I would be asked questions. That was when I realized that something was wrong. He said I could move in with him for a bit. I don't think he really wanted me there but he was scared . . . I heard another man tell him that he'd given the lists to some men in a pub and that they were using them to break into the houses to steal things. He laughed about it and George said it was to cover up what they were doing, but I didn't understand. Then the other man found out I was staying with George and he got very angry.'

'Did you ever hear his name?'

She nodded. 'George called him Joe—not his last name. He came into the other room . . .' She started to cry with her head down and her wet hair fell forward like a curtain. 'He said George had to get rid of me. I thought he was going to kill me and I didn't know what to do.'

She raised her head. 'I think he wanted to do it but George said he'd make sure I went away. I phoned you again but he came in and hit me . . .' Her hands went up to her face, touched the bruise. 'And then George gave me money.'

'I wish you'd told me all this before,' John said. He knew now that she had been dragged into the affair by George Forbes who hadn't minded sleeping with the girl to keep her out of sight, but at the same time he remembered what the girls who worked with her had said. In the beginning she had boasted about her relationship with Forbes while keeping his identity secret, and so she must have enjoyed it for a time. She had brought most of the rest upon herself and caused a great deal of anguish to others.

'Did you hear them discussing why they wanted the lists in the first place?'

She frowned and looked sulky at the same time. 'Not much. I was in the other room and I didn't understand it.'

'Try,' John said impatiently. Mrs McGuire came back with coffee in mugs and he set his down on a table. 'Anything might be important.'

'Whatever it was, they had to hurry. That's why Joe was so angry, because they hadn't much time left . . . and once I heard him swearing about you. He got very angry when George said you were still interfering—I think he made George follow you around—and it was just after that that I ran away.'

'Will she lose her job, Mr Leith?' the mother asked and John felt like saying that she was damn well certain to lose it after all she'd done, but he tried to keep his temper.

'You do realize that I have to trust people who work for me and what you did caused a lot of damage to the reputation of the business?' Bridie nodded but she seemed such a dull-witted girl that John wondered if she really understood or cared. 'So I can't make any promises about your job. I'm glad you're back home safe—it might have turned out very differently. And of course I'll have to let the police know what you have told me.'

That scared her. As he left, her mother followed him. 'I'll see she doesn't get in trouble again. I'll not let her out of my sight,' she said and John looked back at Bridie. Poor stupid girl. Her one brief spell of excitement would probably be her last.

He couldn't resist driving past Lucy Simpson's empty house as he headed for Gumley's home and was tempted to stop and try to get into the place. It was a nice property, typical of the semi-detached Edwardian houses in that area, although the stonework could do with being cleaned. It had been built at a time when land didn't cost the earth and so had generous gardens to the front and rear, with mature trees softening its outline and creating a buffer zone between it and the traffic. He doubted that there was anything of interest inside it now, but he still had that nagging desire to go inside and take a look. What Tollis would call his inexplicable hunches were probably nothing more than sheer curiosity, but there was no doubt that the house had become a magnet.

Garek welcomed him stiffly and then he had to go through the usual procedure of paying a visit to his father-in-law in the overheated sitting-room. The day had turned squally and rain slid down the windows, obscuring the view. It had the effect of isolating the room from the outside world and that in turn made Gumley a focal point. The old man was brighter than the last time John had seen him, more irascible and keen for a verbal battle. Garek took up a position behind Gumley's chair as if to show that nothing had changed.

'Regular visitor now, eh? Without the boy—bring him tomorrow.'

He was like a gnome curled up in the chair, shrunken and shrivelled as if he had no right to be still alive. Sheer malevolence kept his heart beating and despite all that John disliked about the man, he had a grudging admiration for the way he fought to stay alive.

'The boys have to do their own unpacking and I expect they'll be tired after the long journey. I'll try to bring him.' It was an excuse. He wasn't sure that David would be allowed an afternoon off but he resisted every time Gumley tried to apply pressure.

'You will bring him tomorrow?' Gumley's eyes were fixed on him; Garek looked hopeful.

'I'll try to arrange it,' John said. He needed Garek's help and the man was still loyal to Gumley.

'Show him the present,' Gumley said, and Garek fetched an American football and held it out for John to inspect. 'You said no expensive presents—satisfied? The boy shows an interest.'

It was true that American football was the latest craze and the boys were allowed to watch it on television.

'He can play here—out there,' and Gumley waved a hand in the direction of the windows. It was another enticement. First the dog and now the ball. He couldn't claim custody of the boy in the courts, so he was doing it with subtlety and once David saw Garek's collection of Harley bikes it would be an added attraction. John could foresee many visits in future.

'You agree?' Gumley looked disappointed that there was to be no argument.

'I agree. Don't I always, for the sake of peace?'

'Huh,' Gumley growled, no longer interested.

Garek moved away from the chair and motioned for John to follow. They went to the library and John showed him the letter Smith had sent to Maria in Canada.

'Is this the usual sort of thing lawyers send out as a final settlement of the estate?'

Garek nodded. He had showed no reaction to the sums of money mentioned, but then Garek rarely showed anything.

'You can check the figures by visiting the land registration department and the auctioneers will have records of the furniture sales,' he said. Then he drew out a sheet of paper of his own and handed it across to John.

'Alvin's have narrowed Harley owners down to three names and they still hope to eliminate two of them.'

John looked at the names and one jumped out at him. 'No need,' he said. 'That's him.'

Garek looked and smiled slightly. 'I thought so, but that address is out of date. He moved three months ago.'

'You checked?'

Garek nodded slowly. 'He has not been seen by other HOG members in that time either. He has vanished.'

CHAPTER 13

'Do you know anything else about him, his age, what he does for a living?'

Garek looked pained. 'We don't get involved with the personal details of the HOG members—we talk motorbikes. I have not met him, but others say he is a loner.'

'Our doorman said he wore a distinctive watch.'

Garek stood up and fetched a catalogue and together they studied the pages of accessories. 'There,' Garek said. He read the details. 'V-twin Bulova, with Swiss quartz movement . . . It is a popular one. The accessories are expensive. It does put your man into a category, that he can afford such things.'

John flipped through the pages and saw stylish knives that bore the Harley slogan: 'Live to ride, ride to live.'

'He owns a knife too, but not one of these—it was ordinary kitchen tool that he had sharpened for the occasion,'

John murmured. He looked through more pages, at jackets, belt buckles, every conceivable item that could have the Harley logo. 'There's more to owning a bike than I imagined.' He looked up to see Garek smiling.

'When you ride a Harley you don't just turn up, you arrive. Maybe one day you will have your own?'

John stood up and stretched. 'You mean I'm catching the bug—you may be right.'

Garek indicated the lashing rain. 'I was going to take the wraps off the bikes but it is not the right weather—maybe when you come tomorrow with David we will do it then.'

'I only said I'd do my best.'

Garek shook his head. 'Mr Gumley will have taken it as a promise and I think you are a man who keeps them even if you would rather not,' he said shrewdly as he walked with John to the door. 'That house, the one that was sold. You will check who bought it still?'

'Mm. I need some straight facts to offer Chief Inspector Jamieson before he'll take any action. It won't be difficult to find out where Forbes lives, so it's only a matter of time before we get the other man.'

Garek stared at him with his dark expressionless eyes, as if to confirm something he already knew. 'I told Mr Gumley many years ago, when he tried to take David away from you, that you were not the type to give in easily. Now he is beginning to believe me, I think. But be careful with this man who owns a knife. Anyone who carries such a weapon intends to use it if he is cornered.'

'I think you're so right,' John said, remembering the way the man had gripped it the previous night.

He knew before he drove away that he was going back to the Simpson house. The rain clouds made the late afternoon gloomy and with the shelter of the trees around the house, it ought to be easy enough to take a look around. But first he wanted to look at the old address given on the HOG membership list, where the biker had once lived with his mother. He had never seen the man's face but from his voice alone he'd got the impression that the man was in his mid-thirties at least. Living with his mother until recently meant that he was either unmarried or divorced. And in the partnership with Forbes he was the dominant one. Already he was learning a lot about him: that he was violent, and had a temper that made him take unnecessary risks; that he would kill if cornered, as Garek said. He was also obsessional, persistent with his threats, although he must know by now that many people knew as much as John.

So where was he today? John had kept a careful watch but there was no sign of a motorbike—that meant nothing. He had been driven away from Kramer's the previous evening in a car—his or Forbes's? And Bridie had said Forbes had tailed him on the biker's instructions; might still be doing so. Also, the biker knew that his face had not yet been seen, so maybe he would now abandon the biker disguise. He could walk the streets quite openly but it made no difference. *Because now I know who you are; I know your name.*

He stopped the car just short of the house where the man used to live. It was a bungalow, with a tidy garden; the grass square in front of the bay window was neatly edged and he wondered if the biker was a dutiful son who helped his mother with the chores. He was tempted to get out and speak to neighbours, to ask if a motorbike had been there recently, but it would serve no useful purpose at this point. He drove on to the Simpson house and stopped a couple of doors away, sat there for a while just watching the passing traffic. No one showed any interest in him at all. Then he got out, taking a torch with him, and casually walked to the gate, went up the path and around to the back.

The garden here was overcrowded with old shrubs around the washing-green area which had long grass. He couldn't see the houses that backed on to the area, nor could anyone looking from a window see him—and that was what he'd expected. An old lady had lived here for many years and all the plants were mature. With only a housekeeper who was no longer so young, the large garden had been allowed to run wild.

He walked along an uneven brick path to the back door which had two panes of glass, one of which was cracked. He tapped it with the torch and felt it move. A stronger tap removed a section and the loose shards fell inwards to clatter on the kitchen floor. He reached in and turned the large old key.

The door had swollen with the damp weather and it scraped the floor noisily as he pushed it open. The broken glass was carried with it and he didn't bother to close it— better to keep his escape route clear, he thought, just in case.

He knew what he was looking for. When the old lady died, it was likely that Mrs Pearson would stay on, out of friendship, to see that the house was cleared of furniture and she might have been asked by Ambrose Smith to show around prospective buyers. Solicitors often welcomed such help, knowing it meant that the house was kept aired and heated and that a lived-in house sold at a better price than one that smelled of stale air. Part of the procedure of the sale was handing out printed leaflets which gave buyers all the details of the property, including the asking price. John was hoping that some were still lying around.

The kitchen was old-fashioned, with double porcelain sinks and a large water tank on the wall. A couple of cardboard cartons containing newspapers lay on the floor, remnants from packing, perhaps.

It was getting difficult to see much as he went through the rest of the rooms but he didn't want to use the torch until he had to. There was a sitting-room and dining-room downstairs and another smaller room next to a toilet. All were bare and swept clean, as he had expected from a conscientious housekeeper.

Another door showed steps leading down to a cellar that didn't seem to have electric lighting. He did use the torch now, and as he descended he smelled dampness. It was unpleasant, like the smell of open trenches in roadworks, of drains. He stood at the bottom and swung the beam of the torch over the room, which was quite large. To one side were more of the cartons, folded flat and tied with string, and beside them a black plastic sack of rubbish. He laid the torch down and untied the neck of the bag and rummaged around inside.

'Eureka,' he murmured, closing his hand on a bundle of brochures. 'Thank you, Mrs Pearson.' His voice echoed off the bare stone walls as he shone the torch on the first brochure which had a photograph of the house on the front page, with the asking price below it. At the same time he heard soft footsteps overhead as if someone was walking carefully along the hallway. He switched off the torch and held his breath.

The cellar door slammed shut and he distinctly heard the key turn in the lock. Had he been deliberately locked in, or had the person up there automatically shut the door because it opened over dangerously steep stairs? Who was it? His mind raced. Should he call out and reveal himself? He remembered the biker and his knife and decided to keep very quiet. He didn't have long to wait.

'Mr Leith.' The voice was muffled. John stayed where he was, crouched by the plastic bag and didn't answer. Whoever it was couldn't be sure which room he was in.

'Mr Leith, I know you're down there. I saw the light through the grating.'

John glanced up to the grille which would be at garden level, that was letting in some light from the street lamps. He was at the front of the house and his torch beam must have passed over the grating. He stood up and went up the steps, put his ear to the door and could sense that the man was only inches away from him.

'I was following you.'

John concentrated on the voice, heard the nervousness in it and knew that it had to be Forbes.

'It's obvious you know too much if you could find that bungalow . . .' The tone was almost apologetic now, uncertain. 'I think it's best if I keep you here for a while.'

'That's not a good idea—people know what I'm doing, know that I was coming here,' John said, trying to sound calm.

No answer.

'Do you hear me, Forbes—they know I'm here.'

'I'll have to take that chance.'

'But you can't just leave me shut up here. I have no food, no water—how long do you plan to keep me locked in?'

He could almost see Forbes hesitating. When he spoke again his voice was stronger. 'He'll kill you. You'll be safe here. I won't tell him, I promise.'

'Is that supposed to make me feel better? Let me out. You can leave, fly off somewhere. I won't tell the police.'

'I can't. We need a few more days—I don't want anything to happen to you and this is the best answer.'

'I won't last for days down here. It's cold.'

'I'll bring food,' the man said but it had to be a lie. Forbes wouldn't dare open the door again. John heard him move away.

'Forbes! If you're waiting for him to pay you your share you're a fool. You can't trust him.' The footsteps stopped.

'I have to. It all got out of hand and he got angry when you interfered. We hadn't planned to leave yet—it's your own fault, Mr Leith.'

'Why did you do it? You had a good job.'

'I used to have a good job but your uncle changed all that.' He sounded bitter.

'And now you're in this up to your neck—equal partners, equal guilt. The court won't make allowances for you.'

'I haven't done anything so bad—I made that girl go away to somewhere safe.'

'And what about Maria Twarog?' John had his face close to the door, hoping he could keep Forbes there long enough to scare him into unlocking it.

'That had nothing to do with me!'

'Do you think anyone will believe that if you leave me shut in here? You'll rot in gaol for life.'

There was a long silence. Forbes was still there, thinking

it over. Then he spoke with new determination. 'You know too much. If I let you out I will get caught, but in a couple of days we'll be able to leave. You'll have to stay in there.'

This time Forbes did leave and John heard the retreating footsteps, then heard Forbes tugging the back door shut and the crash as more glass fell from the broken panel.

'Shit!' He went back down the stairs and lit the torch. Outside a wind had sprung up and it was still pouring with rain. A little fresh air came in through the grating but it didn't do much to improve the stale air and later he would no doubt curse it for making the cellar even colder.

He sat on the pile of cartons and let the torch beam play over the room again. In one corner there was a heap of coal and on a shelf, covered in cobwebs were some old paint tins and a jar of screws. There was no exit apart from the door and that was solid. He had to think about survival and also be prepared for the weak Forbes breaking his promise and telling the biker that John was trapped.

The facts were that he might be in the cellar for days, that at any time the man with the knife might appear and, most depressing of all, no one knew where he was. He could try shouting through the small grating but that was several feet above his head, and the very seclusion that had let him get into the house secretly, also meant that no one was likely to hear him.

'Brilliant. A mouse couldn't get out.'

Already he was feeling cold and he'd left his outer coat in the car. There was also a warm tracksuit in the boot but a fat lot of use that was now. He tried not to think of the lunch he'd skipped and turned off the torch to save the batteries. The faint light coming through the grating would have to do. He slid the string from the cartons, laid a couple flat on the floor and made up two into large cartons. He now had a bed and if he crept inside the boxes he might retain body heat—if he was there for any length of time.

The next thing was to be ready in case Forbes gave away his presence. He searched every corner of the cellar but the only thing possible as a weapon was the coal.

'So I sit here and throw lumps at him,' he muttered. He sat down and cursed himself for getting into this situation. He looked up at the door which opened inwards, knowing that the screws of the hinges were out of reach on the other side, but the lock was on the inside. Without much hope he ran his hands over the dusty shelf, found a few nails, but nothing resembling a screwdriver. He emptied his pockets and took his bank card out of his wallet, then went up the stairs and tried to ease it behind the bolt of the lock. It worked in films, but this was a much stouter lock and the card simply bent. He sat on the top step and looked down; they were steep and someone coming in wouldn't notice a thin piece of string stretched across at ankle level.

He fetched a long nail from the jar and knocked it into a gap in the panelling on one side of the stairs, tied the string from the cartons around it and looped the other end securely over the handrail on the other side.

'And that's it,' he said. As a defence it was pretty puny, but he would hear anyone approaching along the hall. If the tripwire worked, and if he could surprise whoever entered . . . if, if . . .

He did another tour of the cellar with the torch lit this time and he paused by the heap of coal.

'But how did it get here?' It was unlikely that a coal merchant would heave coal bags right through the house and all the way down those stairs—it was impossible, in fact. Not daring to hope, he pulled at the coal, then scrambled over the heap and kicked it away from the wall. There was a hatch with a door on a swinging hinge that he could just about scramble through and he felt the grime coating him as he slithered under the door and a little way up the slope that ought to lead to the garden.

Rain had seeped in through the top for years to encourage the growth of moss, and mixed with the coal dust it made a slippery climb. Several times he slipped back to the bottom but eventually he got to know where the cracks in the brickwork were and using fingers, knees and toes he reached the top. He felt a stone slab over his head and it was stuck solid. The roots of weeds were growing down around two of its edges and he guessed that Lucy had learned the benefits of central heating and it was a long time since any coal had come down the chute. At one time the opening would have been covered by a simple wooden door, but if he remembered right there was now a wide path of these slabs running under the front bay window.

He was only precariously balanced and had nothing to push against, so he was soon forced to slide back down and crouch at the bottom, gasping for breath. He needed something to make steps or an iron rod to ram into the bricks to stand on, and he had nothing of the kind. For the first time he felt really uneasy. What would it be like if he *was* there for days, a week, or forever? He was filthy and the damp patches on his clothes added to the discomfort, so he crawled to the cardboard refuge and curled up inside.

The hours passed slowly and he ignored hunger and thirst, knowing the worst of them were still to come. At midnight he assumed that Forbes had kept his word, and at that point he tried to sleep. He dozed, waking at the slightest sound. There was the occasional car passing outside but the worst noises were the soft ones, the unidentifiable ones. A small rustle made him jump up in alarm. It was only the sound of the trees moving in the wind but he had to turn on the torch to make sure, shining it in every corner, behind the coal, his flesh creeping at the thought of rats . . .

He was cold as deep as his bones. Rolling the cardboard around his body made no difference, so he exercised, ran on the spot, until his blood warmed and then he tried to sleep again just to make the hours pass more quickly. It was a very long night.

Daylight came, although very little light reached the cellar through the grating, and he crawled up the chute again. He probed the edge of the stone slab with a long nail, holding himself in position with his knees jammed against the opposite wall. The slab was much larger than the opening or it would have fallen in, but it was too heavy to move in any case. He tried the supporting bricks, working on the mortar until he had pulled two loose. There was a compacted layer of rubble behind them composed of large stones. The builder had been conscientious and he swore and slid back to the bottom again.

He took stock. His clothes were torn at knees and elbows and he'd lost a lot of skin but he had to keep trying. For hours he persisted in pulling bricks free from the top of the chute, resting at the bottom and climbing up and doing the same thing all over again. In the middle of the afternoon he had made little progress, was exhausted and desperate for a drink, so he crawled back into the cellar and lay down.

It was the lowest point. He had kept going through anger at first and then with the sheer determination to get out, but now he was beginning to hope that Forbes would break his promise and then the biker would come. He would at least be able to put up a fight . . .

He slept and almost missed the sound of footsteps above. When he opened his eyes he lay still, waiting for the sound of the key in the lock, imagining the figure entering, tripping over the string . . . He jumped up and picked up a lump of coal.

'John?'

He couldn't recognize the voice, didn't answer.

'John Leith?' Louder this time and it sounded like Mike Cairns.

He tried to answer but managed only a croak. Dropping the coal, he ran up the steps, tripped over the string and then pounded on the door. 'In here.'

'There's no key—stand back.'

Mike put his foot to the door and it shuddered. Time after time the big man kicked and at last wood splintered and the lock gave way. The door flew towards John and he climbed the last steps and left the cellar.

Mike stood there looking at him with his mouth open and then his face crumbled. He began to laugh, a deep baritone sound that echoed in the empty house. 'You are filthy.'

'I need something to drink, for God's sake,' John said. Later he might manage to see the funny side of it but now he pushed by Mike and headed for the kitchen. He put his mouth under the tap and drank.

'Now let's get out of here,' he said but Mike looked at him helplessly.

'Like that?'

'If I stain your seat covers I'll buy you new ones, but I'm not hanging around here while you arrange for me to take a bath.'

'The car's at the gate,' Mike said and led the way. They were close to the Botanic Gardens, a favourite place for Sunday afternoon excursions, so his short walk to the car did not go unnoticed, but John didn't care if the Queen herself was watching.

'What made you come here?'

'Gumley's man phoned, said you'd promised to bring David for the afternoon and it bothered him when you failed to turn up. He went and fetched David himself—he's there at Gumley's now.'

'Garek was bothered.' John felt like laughing, it was so typical of the man to understate what could have been a disaster, even if he wasn't to know it. 'He was bothered! You'd better take me there, then,' he said.

'If you insist, but don't expect me to hang around,' Mike said as he swung the car around and headed for Cramond. 'You know how I feel about Gumley.'

'And you haven't explained how you knew where to look,' John reminded him.

'Garek said you seemed intrigued by that house and he suggested I try there first. I spotted where you'd parked the car, so it was easy.' He glanced at John. 'Getting a bit hairy, was it?'

'You could say that.' He didn't feel like expanding on that and Mike didn't ask. 'Do you think my father-in-law will let me take a bath?'

'I think he will insist,' Mike said with a chuckle. 'I wouldn't let you in my house looking like that.'

They entered the driveway and Mike dropped him at the door, then drove away with a wave of his hand. John could see David on the far side of the lawns, entering the shrubbery after the dog, and he was able to slip inside the house without the boy seeing him, which was just as well, he thought ruefully when he saw himself in the bathroom mirror later. And he knew why Mike had laughed. Black from head to foot, his clothes in rags, he hardly recognized himself. He stood there for some time, not at all amused. 'I'll have the last laugh,' he vowed as he stripped and ducked under the shower.

Garek had taken one look at him and led the way upstairs; he provided clothes, a polo-necked black sweater and a tracksuit and also an antiseptic salve that stung like hell. When he was again respectable John joined Garek and Gumley in the sitting-room.

'Explanations later, Mr Leith. Please help yourself,' and Garek indicated a pot of coffee and sandwiches. John ate, ignoring his father-in-law's disapproval. The old man was unusually quiet and John guessed that all the enjoyment of baiting him was gone now that he was treating the house as a second home. Maybe the old man even resented the fact that Garek had another interest, it was hard to tell.

He told the two men what had happened, but kept it brief. 'I don't think I would have got out if you hadn't—'

Garek raised his hand and cut short his thanks.

'Then I'll go talk to my son,' John told him after he'd cleared the plate of food. His body was stiff, the joints of his fingers raw, but he needed to be outside to rid himself of the claustrophobic feeling of the cellar.

'Throw the ball, Daddy.' The American football was tossed across the lawn for half an hour, interspersed with tales of long hikes, of birdwatching, of sausages burned over camp fires.

'I think it's time to take you back to school for tea,' John said at last and his son came running, clutching the ball, his face shining. The dog romped around them. It was good to be free and alive. And come Monday it would all be over and he was looking forward to that with a fierce longing that he recognized as lust for revenge. It was a sweet feeling.

Garek understood. John felt as if the man had somehow become a blood brother and it was the same feeling, only slightly different, that he shared with Clare. She could put into words what he was thinking, startle him with her insight, and in the same way, Garek knew that John was tasting blood.

CHAPTER 14

Garek had suggested leaving John's car outside the Simpson house.

'In case Forbes drives past to see if you are still there— I doubt if he would go inside again.' Then he'd driven David back to school and John to Kramer's. He seemed to be enjoying his part in the proceedings.

John made for Val's office, checked the personnel records for Forbes's address and found that it was still listed. He phoned and left a message for Jamieson, but doubted if he would get much out of the man. Forbes would be too scared to rat on his partner.

Reaction set in. John roamed the small flat restlessly, knowing there was nothing more he could do until the next morning when he would set about proving what the pair had been up to. He wondered what Clare was doing, then picked up the phone and dialled her number and as soon as she answered he knew that she was glad to hear his voice.

'John?'

'I'm missing you,' he said and the urgency was there even though he'd intended to play it cool. The last thing he wanted was for her to feel she was under any pressure.

She didn't answer right away, so he filled the gap. 'When do you leave?'

'Tuesday. I'll be gone about a week. They allow me that

time, with expenses, to look over the new office and find somewhere to stay.'

'When are you coming back?'

'In a week.' Her voice was brittle bright. 'I don't know the exact day, if that's what you mean. It depends on how it goes.'

There was so much he wanted to say but he was afraid she didn't want to hear it. 'I'll see you next week, then,' he said.

'Yes.' It was said softly but he couldn't tell what it meant. Clare was closed right up and was giving nothing away.

'Call me—let me know when . . .'

'I will . . . really, I will.'

Tollis had been true to his word and now the Kramer building had video cameras in the entrance hall, but John didn't sleep any easier because of them. He dreamed of struggling up the dank coal chute and in the small hours he gave up trying to sleep and made himself some tea and toast. He lit the gas fire, remembering the coldness of the cellar where he would still be if it hadn't been for Garek.

He had more or less worked out why the biker had become violent when he found out that John was looking for Bridie and Mrs Pearson, and why everything had escalated when Maria came on the scene, but there were a lot of gaps and he still had to prove what the biker and Forbes were up to.

The two men were on the point of cashing in and then they would leave the country and there was nothing he could do to stop them. He had nothing to tell Chief Inspector Jamieson yet, apart from Bridie's story and the possibility that Forbes had left fingerprints on the handle of the cellar door.

He didn't want Forbes pulled in for any of that. He wanted the weak man to be free to aggravate the biker with his fear and doubts. And Forbes would do that. Maybe Garek was wrong and Forbes would give in to a bout of conscience and go back to Lucy's house to see if John was surviving. Getting no answer, his imagination would work overtime. Forbes wouldn't dare open the cellar door to find out and he would turn to jelly; certainly he would be no help to the biker.

The biker. The name had become real and it conjured up the blankness of his identity behind the visor of the helmet. 'But I know his name, even if I don't know what he looks like,' John muttered. 'And soon I'll come face to face with him.' That was what he wanted most of all.

Despite his snack in the middle of the night, he ate a good breakfast, maybe to make up for the calories he had lost, or to set himself up for a busy day. At 9.30 he left to pay a visit to Meadowbank House where the register of sasines was held. Sasine, a good old Scots word, meant the giving of legal possession of feudal property. He'd had to look it up once rather than let his uncle know his ignorance of the property terms, and he'd been glad that the term was still in use.

The office that was open to the public was busy and John had to wait while a queue of solicitors' messengers were dealt with but he didn't mind because it gave him an idea of how the system worked. Then it was his turn.

'I want to find out who owns a property,' he told the young man at the desk.

'Address?'

John gave it.

'You'll have to go up to the fifth floor to see the search sheet—each floor deals with a different area.'

But first he had to pay a fee and collect a receipt to present to the woman on the fifth floor. She was efficient and quickly brought him a book to study.

'That's the property you want,' she said, pointing to a page. She found him a space at a long table and all around him others were studying similar details in other books. The page in front of him gave a history of all the owners of the house preceding Lucy Simpson. The trouble was that Lucy was still listed as the current owner. He waved to the pleasant woman.

'Is this up-to-date? The house has been sold.'

'How long ago was the sale?'

'At least six months ago, I think.'

'It can take nine months or so before it's entered in the book.' And she explained the various procedures that would eventually result in the new entry reaching the search sheet. 'It would also tell you if any other loans had been taken out, second mortgages and the like. That's what a lot of these people are doing, checking on behalf of lawyers.'

'But the information is in this building somewhere?'

She nodded. 'If the lawyer has got around to sending in the disposition.'

John remembered the messengers on the floor below and decided to go back to square one. The same young man explained what happened when the lawyer sent his messenger along to have the security of a property to be registered.

'The writs are either delivered or posted to us and they are entered in the presentment book. That's this book on the counter which is open to public inspection.' He showed John that day's entries. The name of the lawyer was given, the date, and the name of the grantor or grantee. It occupied a single line and there had already been a great many entries that day.

'Is there any way you can search back to an entry six months ago?'

'Ah no. As you can see there would be thousands.'

'What happens when all the information has been recorded and the information is in the search sheet?'

'The deed is returned to the agent—whoever sold the house on behalf of the owners—and he passes it on to the person lending the mortgage, who holds on to it until the mortgage is repaid.'

One door was closed, John realized as he drove back to the town centre, but there was one more thing he wanted to do that morning. It took him half an hour and then he was heading back to Kramer House. Tollis was busy with the Monday schedules but John was content to wait. He

had a lot of thinking to do. It was after twelve before Tollis
agreed to a snack lunch eaten at his desk.

'I ordered extra sandwiches because Jamieson is coming,'
John said.

'Mm, sounds interesting. Do I get to hear what you've
been up to—apart from getting yourself kidnapped?'

'You heard, then?'

'The whole office knows how Mike found you and the
state you were in. They're taking bets on your next trick.'

'It's—ah—a bit of a long story. We'd better wait for
Jamieson,' John said.

Jamieson was late and Tollis was itching to get back to
work by the time he arrived, but the policeman wasn't
alone.

'I thought it would be best if I brought along a colleague,'
Jamieson explained. 'Superintendent Bill Brown. You don't
mind if he listens in?'

The Superintendent was already sitting down as Tollis
shook his head. Jamieson took the last chair. 'Well, Mr
Leith?' He looked expectant.

'I'd better go back a bit for the sake of . . .'

'Bill,' the new man said.

'I'll start at the point where I got involved, and it began
really, with Maria Twarog. She came over from Canada
for a visit after inheriting some property and she wanted
Sentinel to find the housekeeper, Mrs Pearson, who was
looking after some things for her. I couldn't find her but
the fact that I was searching alarmed two men. One of them
is called Forbes—until recently he worked for Kramer's as
a surveyor—and the other . . . well, I call him the biker
because he rides a Harley Davidson and I've never seen his
face. He tried to warn me off—threatened to kill me if I
didn't stop "interfering".

'He also laid a false trail by getting Bridie McGuire to
copy lists of empty properties—he did need to see those
lists but he passed them on to two young thugs who
promptly burgled the houses. That kept us in the dark for
a while.

'Forbes and the biker were in fact very much afraid that I would eventually ask Maria more about her inheritance and they tried to silence her. One of them ran her down with his car. He also searched her luggage which was in my flat and tampered with my car. What he hoped to find was the letter that Maria had in her bag—which I now have. She suffered brain damage and although she's recovering, she is partially paralysed.'

'We never found the car,' Jamieson put in.

'I think we will though, hidden in a garage,' John said. 'Forbes has been using taxis.'

He went on with the story and the three other men listened intently.

'It was the house that I kept coming back to. It was still empty and it was the only thing that connected Maria to Mrs Pearson, but I couldn't figure out what possible significance it had until I read that final settlement that the lawyer, Ambrose Smith, sent to Maria in Canada. I went into the house hoping to find a sale brochure, and in it the house was for sale at offers over £85,000. Today I went to study the registers of land sales out at Meadowbank.'

Jamieson was nodding as if he had expected to hear this.

'Lucy Simpson is still listed as the owner of the house and it was what I expected to find in a way, but it proved nothing because it takes a while before the information is altered to show the new owner. Then I followed up the only other clue I had.'

'And it paid off, or we wouldn't be here,' Jamieson said. 'What is the result of all of this, Mr Leith?'

'It is obvious that there are not just two men involved in all this, but three.' He took the letter that Maria had given him and handed it to Jamieson, who looked at it, passed it to the Superintendent, while Tollis looked puzzled. He whistled when it was his turn to study the letter.

'You must be wrong,' he said, but Jamieson was smiling.

'No. Ambrose Smith cheated Maria out of quite a lot of money. She received less than forty thousand in total—that includes the sale of the contents, furniture, etc. When I saw those figures I knew he had to be in on it. I went to see the auctioneer who sold the furniture and he has a record of the cheque he gave Smith on Maria's behalf. I spoke to him this morning and he's still feeling put out that he didn't get *all* the furniture to sell. In his words, Lucy must have collected antiques all her life. He was asked to value the contents of the house for Smith and he knew it was normal for the incoming owners to be offered the chance of buying the existing furnishings so he wasn't surprised not to get all of it for sale. But as you can see from that letter, Smith gave Maria less than the auctioneer got for a small portion that he did sell. No wonder Smith was upset when she came to this country. He must have felt safe sending that cheque off to Canada, never guessing she would come here on holiday.'

'And he passed the word to the other two,' Jamieson said.

'I should have guessed sooner,' John admitted. 'On the day that Maria was knocked down, Smith had just asked me for her address—but at the time we did think it was just hit-and-run.'

John looked at Jamieson, noted the smug expression. 'You suspected this, didn't you?'

Jamieson rubbed the back of his neck. 'I've seen it before, which is why I asked Bill to come along. He's in the Fraud Squad.'

'Ambrose Smith,' Tollis said again. He scratched his head. 'Risked everything for a few thousand pounds? And those other two, the threats, the actual violence against that young woman . . .'

For the first time the Fraud Squad man entered the discussion. 'No, not for a few thousand pounds but I'm not going to start speculating on how much he has embezzled over the years—yes, years. This has the classic sound of long-term fraud and his sort of practice—trust funds, looking after old ladies' investments—I've seen it all before. This letter—' he tapped the letter John had given him— 'along with a statement from the auctioneer, is priceless evidence because it is all we need to inform the Law Society. They will send in their investigators but more likely they'll give Smith some warning that they are about to descend on him.'

'Warn him?' Tollis looked astonished but the Superintendent nodded calmly.

'They know what they are about. With any luck he'll panic and try to get rid of incriminating papers, do a cover-up. That makes their job easier. It's surprisingly easy to prove what he's been up to once the suspicion has been raised. And he can't deny it. In the meantime I'll get my lot mobilized. Do you fancy an afternoon with me, Mr Leith?'

John didn't bother to answer, he just grinned.

'The first step,' Bill Brown said as they drove to the town centre, 'is to pay a visit to some building societies. Did you bring a copy of those lists that the young woman copied? I have a feeling we'll hear some interesting answers to the questions I have in mind.'

And for the next two hours John sat in on interviews with the managers of several building societies. The same opening question was asked.

'Have you granted loans on any of these properties?'

In all cases the managers said they were bound by the need for confidentiality, but after Bill Brown convinced them that what they said would be 'off the record', most agreed to cooperate. John listened to the rest with amazement but the Superintendent was only getting the answers he'd obviously expected.

'It's in their own interest after all,' he said grimly as he called a halt to seeing other building society managers. 'There will be a wide sweep now to see who else Smith has got loans from.'

'I can't believe it,' John said. 'I didn't realize that such things could happen.'

'I'm afraid there's more to come,' the policeman said. 'Let's take a quick look at the scene of the crime,' and he parked on double yellow lines outside Smith's office. He strode up the steps purposefully and John doubted if any traffic warden would argue with him about a parking ticket. The man was like a bulldog with his teeth in the seat of someone's pants and he wasn't about to let go.

Smith sat in one of his period chairs, looking sick and deflated. He showed no sign of recognizing John, who doubted if Smith was capable of feeling anything. The man was in shock. Around him the accountants were quietly going about the business of ferreting out his misdeeds, but one broke off to speak to the policeman.

'That's that, then,' Bill said with something close to lip-smacking satisfaction. 'Now we'll go tell Robert Jamieson the good news.' And as they left Smith's place of work, John noted that the secretary was absent, her desk bare. The air of opulence had been exposed as a front for something very tawdry indeed.

'Mortgage fraud,' Jamieson said as they drank a civilized cup of tea in his room.

Bill explained to John. 'I don't know the figures yet for Scotland, but in England last year fraud officers discovered over thirty million had been defrauded by crooked solicitors —and we don't know how much they missed, of course. It happens all the time in any city in the land. In Smith's case it's too early to say but I have a feeling we're talking about millions of pounds, from the early looks of this thing.'

'He'll be arrested?'

'I'll be going to the procurator fiscal today to tell him I have a case to answer. He'll go to the Sheriff and say "I have evidence that a crime has been committed" and bingo! we're in business. Got the bastard. He's nabbed and he knows it.'

'Because Maria came here from Canada?'

'That's how it goes. It is usually something quite small that catches them out. Either they get over-confident, or too greedy. They can't resist a sucker who is an old lady in a home, signing away her power of attorney, or someone like that young girl who would be delighted with her inheritance, never dreaming he only gave her less than half. I hate the buggers and that's why I get job satisfaction.'

'But how? How did he get away with it?'

'Lucy Simpson's house, those on your lists that are empty, any property he fancied, Smith took out mortgages on them, sometimes three or four from different building societies *on the same house*. He had bogus survey reports done by Forbes and applied for loans on behalf of non-existent clients, and didn't send any securities to Meadowbank House, of course. No property sales were registered, and for nine months or so no one suspects him as long as he keeps up the interest payments. If a building society begins to ask questions like "Where are the deeds on that property on which we lent a mortgage?" he pays off the loan and begins again. It takes a cool mind and not a lot of juggling. But you, Mr Leith, made things suddenly too hot for them.' He grinned and Jamieson smiled benignly.

'They planned one last scam and got Bridie McGuire to steal those lists. Then they were going to cash in and fly away to a sunny land.'

Jamieson was nodding. 'As soon as I heard that Forbes was a surveyor . . . well, the two always go together, a crooked lawyer is nearly always tied in with a valuer. I haven't got Forbes yet, by the way. He hasn't been near his flat all day.'

'The biker,' John said. 'Where does he fit?'

'The strong man to keep the others in line. Smith apparently has been bleating that he was blackmailed and forced to continue because of your biker friend—who first suggested the whole thing to Forbes. That won't wash in court, though. For one thing he kept the other two informed—including passing on Maria's address.'

'I know who the biker is now,' John said. 'His name is Joseph Pearson and he's the housekeeper's nephew. Smith knew all along where she was living but when I began to ask questions . . . no wonder he acted the way he did. They sent her off on holiday because if I'd talked to her I'd have discovered her nephew had a Harley. Maybe Joseph Pearson dipped into his profits to get her out of the way. It would sound reasonable to her. Her brother had died and

she is offered a holiday with the widow—a kind act as far
as she's concerned. She'll be due back soon.'

'And they'll know we're still looking for her. She knew
how much the house was selling for because Smith went
through all the normal procedures, advertising, etcetera, in
case neighbours got suspicious. If she's due back, that's
their deadline. It's time I got a move on,' the Superintendent said. 'Thank you very much, Mr Leith.'

'A job well done,' Jamieson said, after the Superintendent
had gone, but John knew it was too soon to pat each other
on the back. The main character was still missing.

'I have a feeling it's not over yet,' John said. 'And I won't
relax until I know Pearson is behind bars. Just make sure
you get him.'

CHAPTER 15

Tollis was still dumbfounded about Smith's involvement.
'No one in their right mind would connect that man with
fraud. He's so . . .'

'Paternal, respectable, a pillar of society?' John teased.

'So I was wrong, but a lot of people are going to be
shocked. Wait until this hits the news stands.'

'And I didn't consider he was bent either, not until last
weekend and even then . . . I just didn't like him.'

Tollis wasn't sure about that. 'It's like Jamieson's itch.
You have the same gift for sniffing out the phonies. With
practice you might learn to recognize it sooner. You've done
well for Sentinel, young John. You'll be an asset.'

'No. I'm not going on the payroll. Rees's business has
become my baby and I want to see it through its teething
troubles. And it's going to take time to settle down because
I'm not Rees. Gumley pointed that out. Besides, it's a whole
lot safer.'

Tollis snorted. 'If safe is what you want, you're kidding
yourself. You may have given up on Sentinel but I doubt

if it has given up on you. Let's have a Scotch to celebrate.'

Jamieson called later to say that Forbes had been picked up. 'We found a Volvo with a damaged wing in his garage but he swears he wasn't driving it when it hit Miss Twarog. Maybe he's telling the truth but for the moment we're letting him worry a bit.'

'What about Pearson?'

'No trace of him and Forbes clams up as soon as the name is mentioned. He's shit-scared of the man. I think Forbes was under pressure to do just as he was told and there was a bit of greed involved to keep him going. He hasn't got much out of it so far, according to him, but that doesn't mean he isn't as guilty as the others. I'll want a comprehensive statement from you soon.'

Which would include telling about Forbes's turning of the key in the cellar door. John didn't feet a twinge of sympathy for him, but knew that he had to tell Val what was happening to her ex-husband.

She took the news calmly. If anything her tension of the past week seemed to evaporate. 'It's no more than he deserves,' she said, and John knew that she was thinking of the way her husband had abandoned her when her child was found to be abnormal. 'I'm glad he's out of my life.' It was likely to be the last time Forbes would ever be mentioned as far as she was concerned and later he heard her humming to herself.

Tollis rarely came up to the Kramer floor but that evening he appeared and leaned against the door frame. 'Did you say Mrs Pearson had moved in with her sister-in-law here in Edinburgh?'

'Mm. The biker's mother.'

'Does Jamieson have that address?'

'I forgot to mention it. I checked and there's no one there . . . you think he'd go back there?'

Tollis shrugged. 'I doubt it. If he's trying to liquidate his assets, he'd be a fool to show himself where he's known, but he doesn't strike me as being too sensible. I've met men like him before, who think they'll never be caught, that they're invulnerable, and he would feel safe in his old home. Maybe for a few hours until he can slip away on that motor-bike of his.' Tollis grinned. 'You've had all the fun so far —fancy taking a look?'

John's first instinct was to refuse. He didn't want to stand between Joseph Pearson and freedom, but on the other hand, with Tollis along . . .

'I'll come for you around nine, but get rid of the white shirt,' Tollis said. 'Put on something dark and I'll bring a few things from downstairs.'

They shouldn't be doing this, John thought later as he pulled on a dark sweater over jeans, slid his feet into black running shoes, but he went to join Tollis all the same and together the two men walked out into a chilly night. John looked up at the clear sky and knew that there would be a frost later and the next morning would be crisp and ideal for running.

'Stargazing?'

John slid into the car and reached for the seat-belt. 'Just planning what I'll do tomorrow, if I'm still around.' He felt a shiver run down his spine as he said it.

Tollis too looked serious. 'I'm not underestimating him,' he said as he let in the clutch. 'We're not going to take any chances. If there's any sign of him in that house we'll send for the cavalry.'

The bungalow looked as empty as it had the last time John had visited it. They parked at a safe distance and Tollis lit a cigarette as they kept watch but there was no sign of movement, no light in the house.

'There's a garage,' Tollis said after a while. 'It wouldn't hurt to take a look through that small window to see if his bike's there.'

He undid his belt and let it slide free. 'Come on. If the bike is there and if he's as fanatical about his precious Harley as you say—we'll know he has to come back for it.'

With a lot of foreboding John followed Tollis across the street and up the side of the house to the wooden garage. Tollis produced a pencil torch and shone it through the window, shielding even that small beam from the street. John saw the skeletons of dead insects caught in cobwebs and nothing else, and it seemed that Tollis was none the wiser either. 'There's something in there covered in tarpaulin but I can't see the whole shape—to hell with it, I'm going inside.'

There was a heavy padlock on the door but that posed no problem for the slender key that Tollis inserted and the door opened on oiled hinges. John knew right away that under the wrap there was a motorbike but Tollis pulled the cover from it anyway.

'Nice. This is the sportster, then?' He was so casual as he ran his hands over the machine that he was like a man in a showroom inspecting a possible purchase, but John felt as if a cold draught was blowing on the back of his neck and he wanted to get back to the safety of the car. Tollis replaced the cover. Closed the door and then snapped the padlock back on. 'Now we know it's here we can wait a bit longer.'

They returned to the car but Tollis coasted further along the street, pulled up facing the bungalow and on the same side of the street.

'I'll bet he's got a bag inside the house all packed and ready for the off,' he said as he slid down in his seat and relaxed. 'Get your head down below seat level in case he spots the car.'

John was sure that after a while Tollis fell asleep. The big man had his eyes shut and his breathing was deep and regular, but he was always able to catnap at any time. John found it impossible to relax, partly because his long legs were cramped, partly because his nerves were at stretching-point. What the hell were they supposed to do if Pearson showed up?

The street was a quiet backwater with most of the houses looking as if they were owned by pensioners. No children had been out to play, no dogs roamed the gardens, only an occasional car passed along under the shadows of the trees on the other side. He raised his head slightly and looked at the green area which had an iron fence around it. A small private park, probably. There were several dotted around the city, cared for by local residents who paid the gardeners.

He shifted position, eased a crick in his neck, and Tollis squinted his eyes open. 'Anything happening?'

'There's a cloud drifting over the moon.'

'Don't get poetical on me.' He settled down again.

'How long do we sit here?'

'Have you anything better to do?'

Clare would be packing her bags, taking a long soak in the bath, but no, she would not be expecting him to call.

'No,' he said.

'I thought so,' Tollis said.

Another hour passed and it was getting very cold and John was becoming convinced that Pearson had never intended coming back for his bike. He would surely guess that the bike was now a giveaway and that no one had an accurate description of him. Why would he risk showing himself?

It was nearly midnight and most of the lights in the houses had gone out. More clouds had drifted across the moon and since the old-fashioned street lighting was only on one side of the street it was very dark. If Pearson did walk along the dark side they might not see him because of other cars parked there. John eased himself up to take a look and Tollis sighed and opened his eyes.

'All right. We'll go,' he said. 'But it was worth a try.'

He reached for the ignition but at that moment a taxi drew up at the end of the street and a man jumped out and paid the driver.

'Hang on. Let's see where he goes,' Tollis said, alert now.

The man chose the dark side and they caught an occasional glimpse of him. He was taking his time. John felt a familiar tightening of the flesh of his face and his hands became clammy. He could sense Tollis becoming tense too, and without speaking, both slid down in their seats again. They would no longer be able to see the man unless he crossed the road. He did.

'It's him,' Tollis breathed. 'He's heading for the house.'

Was he? The man walked lightly on the balls of his feet, rolling them to keep sound to a minimum and all the time his eyes scanned the street, in front of him and behind. He was big and heavy, dressed in a black bomber jacket and dark trousers. His hands were in his pockets, his face a strange shade of orange as he passed under a light; longish dark hair gleaming as if it was oiled. He looked like a casual walker, a man out for a breath of air, but the watchers in the car knew that he was tensely looking for signs of surveillance.

He moved quickly as he reached the side of the bungalow. One moment he was there, the next he'd vanished into the shadows. Tollis rolled down his window and they heard the faint sound of a door closing but no light came on inside the house.

'Shouldn't we phone Jamieson?' John said.

'Yes.' Tollis turned his head. 'But do you really want to?'

'Mm. No.' It had only taken a moment's hesitation but his answer had been the truth. He was curious, wanted to see what Pearson was going to do and they were safe in the car. They could follow Pearson when he left, or just drive off if it became necessary.

Pearson left the house, the door closed and his dark shape moved to the garage. Keys jingled, the padlock was off the garage door.

Tollis chuckled deep in his chest. 'Now for some fun,' he said and before John could ask him what that meant, he saw Pearson come out of the garage and stand at the top of the path, looking up and down the street. Then he turned and went back inside the garage.

Tollis closed the window tight. 'Be careful now,' he murmured.

John soon found out why. Pearson came striding into sight and he was swinging something that glinted dully in the poor lighting. He came straight for their car and John could feel Tollis's body tense, coil up ready to spring.

'What the hell—' he started to say but there was no time

to wonder, no time to do anything, because Pearson was running at them. He swung his arms back and as he brought them forward John saw the head of the axe aimed at the side window where Tollis sat.

'Oh, Christ.' He was already moving, was half out of the door when Tollis swung his door open, rammed it hard against Pearson. It stopped him in his tracks and he fell sideways, recovered quickly and came behind the car. The back windscreen shattered.

In the midst of it, Tollis had yelled with pain and was now half out of the car, immobile. John reached into the glove compartment, grabbed the first thing that his fingers closed on and stepped out just as Pearson reached him. The heavier man's face was twisted with rage and hatred, maniacal, his hands hung by his side, the head of the axe rested on the ground. They stood there, Pearson breathing heavily and John frozen, wondering how badly Tollis was hurt.

'Leith.' Pearson breathed the word, savoured it, and then bent slightly to put both hands on the shaft of the axe. The blade began to rise. 'I'm going to slice you into little pieces,' he said as the axe head rose to shoulder height. His mouth was gaping wide in a delighted grimace as John pressed the plunger on the aerosol can and sprayed it right into Pearson's face. The jet of chemicals went to its target but Pearson must have inhaled most of it and the effect was immediate. He doubled up but the downward swing of the axe could not be halted and the shaft took John just below the shoulder. His left arm went numb.

Pearson fell on his side in the roadway, curled in a ball, clutching his throat, coughing and gasping for air. It was frightening to watch the man's face darken with his tongue jutting out, his eyes bulging. John didn't remember reaching for the axe, didn't release his grip on it until it became obvious that Pearson was not going to get up again. He tried to see what had happened to Tollis.

'Are you all right?' he asked with a quick glance over his shoulder.

'Bloody door came back on my ankle. I think it's broken. It's OK. I've got a car phone.'

'You had a car phone all the time!' They were sitting in the Royal's accident unit, Tollis in a wheelchair, clutching a brown envelope containing his X-rays.

'I did ask and you didn't want to phone the police,' he said with a grin.

'I thought we'd have to go looking for one, didn't I?'

'How's Pearson?'

They'd all come in the same ambulance but Pearson had been in no condition to threaten anybody.

'They rushed him away. I think his lungs were full of the stuff. It was the de-icer can I picked up.'

'Huh. You did the best thing at the time. He meant to use that axe on us after all.'

'Why didn't he just go? What made him come charging out at us like that?'

'He couldn't get his bike to start,' Tollis said. 'I did a little bit of vandalism.'

'You mucked about with his Harley? No wonder he picked up an axe.'

The nurse came to wheel Tollis to the plaster room and John saw Jamieson come through the doors. He spotted Tollis leaving and then came to stand over John. He looked very angry.

'What now, Mr Leith? If this goes on I'll have to move back to the city to live.'

John began to explain yet again. He seemed to spend a great deal of his time explaining things to the Chief Inspector.

Two weeks later John was on the phone, discussing plans for the weekend with Clare while waiting for Jamieson to arrive. She had come back from London with a clear vision of her future and almost accepting that Sentinel was likely to play some part in his.

'I had time to think,' she'd said calmly.

And he'd told her the decisions he'd made, about swapping his large office for Val's smaller one. 'She will be officially in charge—she has been for months anyway.'
'Will David be home for the weekend?' she asked now. 'We could go to Elmwood and be lazy.'
It was settled and he put the phone down. She planned to come back from London for most weekends, work permitting. It sounded feasible, but . . . Things were changing all around and if he had a crystal ball that would let him see into the future, he didn't think he would want to look in it.
Val put her head around the door. 'That policeman has arrived. They're waiting for you downstairs.'

'Just to round things off,' Jamieson said. 'As Bill Brown said, it was mortgage fraud and embezzlement. Big money.'
He explained. 'Any solicitor can arrange loans, because the building societies are very trusting, as long as he's a member of the Law Society and protected by their indemnity insurance. Forbes was a valuer and provided suitable reports on the properties for him. He had three separate loans out on that house left to Miss Twarog.'
'Three?'
'The building societies don't ask questions of a reputable lawyer, Mr Leith, and they know that there are delays in getting the deeds—if the lawyer is overworked, or if the people at Meadowbank House are still running months behind. It all works in his favour.'
'Incredible,' John said. 'And if he wasn't caught on something like Maria's case? That was a fluke, after all.'
'In theory he could get away with mortgage fraud forever. The building societies will tell you that there is as yet no safe way to stop it, that it needs an industry initiative rather than action by individual societies, but they aren't the losers. They get their money back from the indemnity fund. Smith, of course, was cheating on trust funds too, and he also took the choice antique pieces from Lucy Simpson's house.' Jamieson's mouth showed his disgust. 'The man is beyond words.

'We shouldn't have to rely on accidents to catch people like him. Something as small as a building society sending out a letter that is returned can start it off—a sharp-eyed clerk might begin to wonder. Usually the crooked solicitors overstretch themselves or get careless, and then we discover that they have used such names as Jones or Brown on every application—then you know that they have not been all that ingenious after all.' He paused. 'Smith handled the Kramer affairs, didn't he?'

'We have our own financial department—he couldn't touch our funds. How is Smith taking all this?' John couldn't imagine the man in a cell.

'He's completely shattered. His castle has crumbled after all and he has lost everything, but we may never recover the bulk of it. And he won't be the last one to try it, either.'

'Pearson?' John said and Jamieson nodded, understanding that he had a special interest in him.

'A different sort altogether.' Jamieson looked grim. 'He hasn't fully recovered physically but in any case there is some doubt about his sanity. I think you can rest assured that he will be locked away for the rest of his life.'

'And Maria—will she ever get back what Smith stole?'

'It may take some time to sort out, but yes, she'll recover it all.'

So. It was finished.

After Jamieson had gone Tollis poured them both a large whisky. 'What are you doing this weekend?'

'Clare's getting set for the London job, so we're going to Elmwood for a break. David will be home too, and Maria is making progress so if the doctors give the go-ahead we'll take her with us. We're going to lie about and be generally lazy.'

He wasn't sure if Tollis had even listened to his answer. 'Still thinking about Smith?'

Tollis nodded. 'Did you see the report of his arrest in the paper? He hasn't been using his full name. It's Ambrose Spencer-Smith. Wonder what those initials did for him at his private school? Bet they called him Asshole, and now he's lived up to it, hasn't he?'

He raised his glass. 'Cheers.'